ISBN 978-1-330-51154-1
PIBN 10071815

1 MONTH OF
FREE
READING

at

www.ForgottenBooks.com

By purchasing this book you are eligible for one month membership to ForgottenBooks.com, giving you unlimited access to our entire collection of over 1,000,000 titles via our web site and mobile apps.

To claim your free month visit:
www.forgottenbooks.com/free71815

AND THE

SPANIARDS

BY

EDMONDO DE AMICIS,

AUTHOR OF " HOLLAND," "CONSTANTINOPLE," ETC.

TRANSLATED FROM THE TENTH EDITION OF THE ITALIAN BY

STANLEY RHOADS YARNALL, M. A.

ILLUSTRATED.

IN TWO VOLUMES.

VOL. II.

THE INTERNATIONAL PRESS
THE JOHN C. WINSTON CO.
PHILADELPHIA

CONTENTS.

LIST OF ILLUSTRATIONS.

VOLUME II.

ARANJUEZ.

ARANJUEZ.

As on arriving at Madrid by way of the north, so
on leaving it by way of the south, one must pass
through a desolate country that resembles the poorest provinces of Arragon and Old Castile. There
are vast plains, parched and yellow, which look as
though they would echo like a hollow passageway if
one were to strike them, or crumble like the crust
of a crisp tart. And through the plains are scattered a few wretched villages of the same color as
the soil, which seem as though they would take fire
like a pile of dry leaves if one were to touch a torch
to the corner of one of the huts. After an hour of
travel my shoulders sought the cushions of the carriage, my elbow sought for a support, my head
sought my hand, and I fell into a deep sleep like a
member of Leopardi's " Assembly of Listeners." A
few minutes after I had closed my eyes I was rudely
awakened by a desperate cry from the women and
children, and leaped to my feet, demanding of my
neighbors what had occurred.

But before I had ended my question a general
burst of laughter reassured me. A company of

huntsmen, scattered over the plain, on noticing the approach of the train, had planned to give the travellers a little scare. At that time there was a rumor that a band of Carlists had appeared in the vicinity of Aranjuez. The huntsmen, pretending to be the vanguard of the band, had given a loud shout while the train was passing, as if to call the great body of their comrades to their assistance, and as they shouted they went through the motions of firing at the railway-carriages; hence arose the fright and the cries of my fellow-travellers. And then the huntsmen suddenly threw the butts of their guns into the air to show that it was all a joke.

When the alarm, in which I too shared for a moment, had subsided, I fell once more into my academic doze, but was again awakened in a few moments in a manner much more pleasant than on the first occasion.

I looked around: the vast barren plain had been transformed as by magic into a great garden full of the most charming groves, traversed in all directions by wide avenues, dotted with country-houses and cottages festooned with verdure; here and there the sparkling of fountains, shady grottoes, flowering meadows, vineyards, and bridle-paths—a verdure, a freshness, a vernal odor, an atmosphere of happiness and peace, that enchanted the soul. We had arrived at Aranjuez. I left the train, walked up a beautiful avenue shaded by two rows of noble trees, and after a few steps found myself in front of the royal palace.

The minister Castelar had written in his memorandum a few days before that the fall of the ancient Spanish monarchy was predoomed on that day when a mob of the populace, with curses on their lips and hatred in their hearts, had invaded the palace of Aranjuez to disturb the majestic repose of their sovereigns. I had reached that square where on the 17th of March, 1808, occurred those events which were the prologue of the national war, and, as it were, the first word of the death-sentence of the ancient monarchy. My eyes quickly sought the windows of the apartments of the Prince of Peace; I imagined him, as he fled from room to room, pale and distracted, searching for a hiding-place as the echo of the cry followed him up the stairs; I saw poor Charles IV., as with trembling hands he placed the crown of Spain on the head of the prince of the Asturias; all the scenes of that terrible drama were enacted in fancy before my eyes, and the profound silence of the place and the sight of that palace, closed and desolate, sent a chill to my heart.

The palace has the appearance of a castle: it is built of brick, with trimmings of light stone, and covered with a tile roof. Every one knows that it was built for Philip II. by the celebrated architect Herrera, and that it was adorned by all the later kings, who made it their summer residence. I enter: the interior is magnificent; there is the stupendous reception-hall of the ambassadors, the beautiful Chinese cabinet belonging to Charles V., the marvellous dressing-chamber of Isabella II., and a profusion of the most precious ornaments. But all the riches of the palace are as nothing to the beauty of the gardens. The expectation is not disappointed.

The gardens of Aranjuez (Aranjuez is the name of a little town which lies a short distance from the palace) seem to have been laid out for a race of Titan kings, to whom the royal parks and gardens of our country would have seemed like the flower-beds on their terraces or the plots before their stables. Endless avenues, bordered by trees of measureless height with arched branches interlacing as if bent toward each other by contrary winds, extend in every direction like a forest whose boundaries one cannot see, and through this forest the Tagus, a wide, swift stream, flows in a majestic curve, forming here and there cascades and lakes: an abundant and luxuriant vegetation springs up amid a labyrinth of bypaths, crossways, and sylvan glades; and in every part gleam statues, vases, columns, and fountains rising to a great height and falling in spray, festoons, and drops of water, placed in the midst of all manner of flowers from Europe and America; and, mingling with the majestic roar of the cascades of the Tagus, a flood of song from innumerable nightingales, which make the mys-

terious gloom of the lonely paths ring with their mellow notes. In the depths of the gardens rises a small marble palace of modest proportions which contains all the wonders of the most magnificent royal abode; and here one may still breathe, so to speak, the air of the inmost life of the kings of Spain. Here are the small secret chambers whose ceilings one may touch with the hand, the billiard-room of Charles IV., his cue, the cushions embroidered by the hands of his queens, the musical clocks which enlivened the playtime of his children, the narrow staircases, the little windows about which cluster a hundred traditions of princely caprices, and, finally, the richest retiring-room in Europe, created at a whim of Charles V., containing in itself alone sufficient riches to adorn a palace, without depriving it of the noble primacy which it proudly holds among all other cabinets designed for the same use. Beyond this palace and all around the groves extend vineyards and olive-groves and orchards of fruit-bearing trees and smiling meadows. It is a veritable oasis in the midst of the desert—an oasis which Philip II. chose to create on a day when he was in good humor, as if to enliven with one cheerful image the black melancholy of the Escurial. On returning from the little marble palace toward the great royal palace through those endless avenues, in the shade of those noble trees, in that profound forest silence, I thought of the splendid trains of ladies and cavaliers who once wandered about in the footsteps of the gay young monarchs or the capricious and dissolute queens to the sound of amorous music and songs which told of the grandeur and glory of unconquered Spain; and I sadly repeated with the poet, Ricanati,

> . .. "All is peace and silence,
>   And their names are no longer heard."

But as I looked at those marble seats, half hidden in the shrubbery, and fixed my eyes on the shadow of certain distant paths, and thought of those queens, those lovers, and those mad pranks, I could not refrain from a sigh, which was not one of pity, and a secret sense of bitterness stung me to the heart; and I said, like poor Adan in the poem *Diablo Mundo*, "How are these grand ladies made? How do they live? What do they do? Do they talk, make love, and enjoy like us?" And I left for Toledo, imagining the love of a queen like a young adventurer of the Arabian Nights.

TOLEDO.

TOLEDO.

WHEN one approaches an unknown city one ought to have near by some one who has already seen it and is able to indicate the opportune moment to put one's head out of the window and get the first view. I. had the good fortune to be informed in time. Some one said to me, "There is Toledo!" and I sprang to the window with an exclamation of wonder.

Toledo rises on a sheer rocky height, at whose foot the Tagus describes a grand curve. From the plain one sees only the rocks and the walls of the fortress, and beyond the wall the tips of the belfries and the towers. The houses are hidden from view; the city seems to be closed and inaccessible, and presents the appearance of an abandoned stronghold rather than of a city. From the walls to the river-banks there is not a single house nor tree; all is bare, parched, craggy, precipitous; not a soul is in sight; you would say that to make the ascent it would be necessary to climb, and it seems that at the first appearance of a man on the face of those rocks a shower of arrows would fall upon him from the top of the wall.

You leave the train, get into a carriage, and arrive at the entrance of a bridge. It is the famous bridge Alcantara, which spans the Tagus, surmounted by a beautiful Moorish gate in the form of a tower, which gives it a bold, severe appearance. Crossing the bridge, you turn into a wide roadway which winds up in large serpentine curves until it reaches the top of the mountain. Here it really seems that you are under a fortified city of the Middle Ages, and you imagine yourself in the guise of a Moor or a Goth or a soldier of Alfonso VI. From every part precipitous rocks hang over your head, crumbling walls, towers, and the ruins of ancient bastions, and higher up the last wall which encircles the city, black, crowned with enormous battlements, opened here and there by great breaches, behind which the imprisoned houses rear their heads; and as you climb higher and higher the city seems to draw back and hide itself. Halfway up the ascent you come to the *Puerto del Sol*, a jewel of Moorish architecture, consisting of two embattled towers which are joined over a very graceful double-arched colonnade, under which runs the ancient street; and from that point, if you look back, you may see at a glance the Tagus, the valley, and the hills. You go on and find other walls and other ruins, and finally the first houses of the city.

What a city! At the first moment I caught my breath. The carriage had turned down a little

street, so narrow that the hubs of the wheels almost touched the walls of the houses.

"Why do you turn in here?" I asked the driver.

He laughed and answered, "Because there is no wider street."

"Is all Toledo like this?" I asked again.

"It is all like this," he replied

"Impossible!" I exclaimed.

"You will see," he added.

To tell the truth, I did not believe him. I entered a hotel, dropped my valise in a room, and ran head-long down the stairs to take a look at this very strange city. One of the hotel-porters stopped me at the door and asked with a smile,

"Where are you going, *caballero*?"

"To see Toledo," I replied.

"Alone?"

"Yes; why not?"

"But have you ever been here before?"

"Never."

"Then you cannot go alone."

"And why not?"

"Because you will get lost."

"Where?"

"As soon as you go out."

"For what reason?"

"The reason is this," he answered, pointing to a wall on which hung a map of Toledo. I approached and saw a network of white lines on a black background that seemed like one of those flourishes which schoolboys make on their slates to waste the chalk and vex their teacher.

"No matter," said I; "I am going alone, and if I get lost, let them come and find me."

"You will not go a hundred steps," observed the porter.

I went out and turned down the first street I saw, so narrow that on extending my arms I touched both walls. After fifty paces I turned into another street, narrower than the first, and from this passed into a third, and so on.

I seemed to be wandering not through the streets of the city, but through the corridors of a building, and I went forward, expecting momentarily to come out into an open place. It is impossible, I thought, that the whole city is built in this manner; no one could live in it. But as I proceeded the streets seemed to grow narrower and shorter; every moment I was obliged to turn; after a curving street came a zigzag one, and after this another in the form of a hook, which led me back into the first, and so I wandered on for a little while, always in the midst of the same houses. Now and then I came out at a crossway where several alleys ran off in opposite directions, one of which would lose itself in the dark shadow of a portico, another would end blindly in a few paces against the wall of a house, a third in a short distance would descend, as it were, into the bowels of the earth, while a fourth would clamber up a steep hill; some were hardly wide enough to give a man passage; others were confined between two walls without doors or windows; and all were flanked by buildings of great height, between whose roofs one could see a narrow streak of sky.

One passed windows defended by heavy iron bars, great doors studded with enormous nails, and dark courtyards. I walked for some time without meeting anybody, until I came out into one of the principal streets, lined with shops and full of peasants, women, and children, but little larger than an ordinary corridor. Everything is in proportion to the streets: the doors are like windows, the shops like niches, and by glancing into them one sees all the secrets of the house—the table already spread, the babies in the cradle, the mother combing her hair, and the father changing his shirt; everything is on the street, and it does not seem like a city, but like a house containing a single great family.

I turned into a less-frequented street, where I heard only the buzzing of a fly; my footsteps echoed to the fourth story of the houses and brought some old women to the windows. A horse passes; it seems like a squadron; everybody hurries to see what is going on. The least sound re-echoes in every direction; a book falls in a second story, an old man coughs in a courtyard, a woman blows

her nose in some unknown place; one hears
everything.

Sometimes every sound will suddenly cease; you
are alone, you see no sign of life: you seem to be
surrounded by the houses of witches, crossways
made for conspirators, blind alleys for traitors, narrow doorways suitable for any crime, windows for the
whispers of guilty lovers, gloomy doorways suggest-
ive of blood-stained steps. But yet in all this labyrinth of streets there are no two alike; each one
has its individuality: here rises an arch, there a
column, yonder a piece of statuary. Toledo is a
storehouse of art-treasures. Every little while the
walls crumble, and there are revealed in every part
records of all the centuries—bas-reliefs, arabesques,
Moorish windows, and statuettes. The palaces have
doorways defended by plates of engraved metal, historical knockers, nails with carved heads, 'scutcheons
and emblems; and they form a fine contrast to the
modern houses painted with festoons, medallions,
cupids, urns, and fantastic animals.

But these embellishments detract in no way from
the severe and gloomy aspect of Toledo. Wherever
you look you see something to remind you of the
city fortified by the Arabs; however little your imagination may exert itself, it will succeed in rear-
ranging from the relics scattered here and there the
whole fabric of that darkened image, and then the
illusion is complete: you see again the glorious

Toledo of the Middle Ages, and forget the solitude and silence of its streets. But it is a fleeting illusion, and you soon relapse into sad meditation and see only the skeleton of the ancient city, the necropolis of three empires, the great sepulchre of the glory of three races. Toledo reminds you of the dreams which come to young men after reading the romantic legends of the Middle Ages. You have seen many a time in your dreams dark cities encircled by deep moats, frowning walls, and inaccessible rocks; and you have crossed those drawbridges and entered those tortuous, grass-grown streets, and have breathed that damp, sepulchral, prison air. Well, then, you have dreamed of Toledo.

The first thing to see, after making a general survey of the city, is the cathedral, which is justly considered one of the most beautiful cathedrals in the world. The history of this cathedral, according to popular tradition, dates from the times of the apostle Saint James, first bishop of Toledo, who selected the place where it should be erected; but the construction of the edifice as it appears to-day was begun in 1227, during the reign of San Fernando, and was ended after twenty-five years of almost continuous labor. The exterior of this immense church is neither rich nor beautiful, as is that of the cathedral of Burgos. A little square extends in front of the façade, and is the only place from which one can get

a view of any considerable part of the building. It
is entirely surrounded by a narrow street, from
which, however much you may twist your neck, you
can see only the high outer walls which enclose the
church like a fortress. The façade has three great
doorways, the first of which is named *Pardon*, the
second *Inferno*, and the third *Justice*. Over it rises
a substantial tower which terminates in a beautiful
octagonal cupola. Although in walking around the
building one may have remarked its great size, on
first entering one is struck by a profound sense of
wonder, which quickly gives place to another keen
sense of pleasure, the result of the freshness, the
repose, the soft shadow, and the mysterious light
which steals through the stained glass of innumerable windows and breaks in a thousand rays of blue,
golden, and rosy light which glides here and there
along the arches and columns like the bands of a
rainbow. The church is formed of five great naves
divided by eighty-eight enormous pilasters, each of
which is composed of sixteen turned columns as
close together as a bunch of spears. A sixth nave
cuts the other five at right angles, extending from
the great altar to the choir, and the vaulted roof of
this principal nave rises majestically above the
others, which seem to be bowing to it as if in
homage. The many-colored light and the clear
tone of the stone give the church an air of quiet
cheerfulness which tempers the melancholy appear-

ance of the Gothic architecture without depriving it
of its austere and serious character. To pass from
the streets of the city to the naves of this cathedral
seems like coming out of a dungeon into an open
square: one looks around, draws a deep breath, and
begins to live again.

The high altar, if one wished to examine it minutely, would require as much time as the interior
of a church: it is itself a church—a miracle of little
columns, statuettes, traceries, and ornaments of endless variety, creeping along the iron frames, rising
above the architraves, winding about the niches,
supporting one another, climbing and disappearing,
presenting on every side a thousand outlines, groups,
combinations, effects in gilding and color, every sort
of grace that art can devise—giving to the whole an
effect of magnificence, dignity, and beauty. Opposite the high altar rises the choir, divided into three
orders of stalls, marvellously carved by Philip of
Bourgogne and Berruguete, with bas-reliefs representing historical events, allegories, and sacred legends—one of the most famous monuments of
art.

In the centre, in the form of a throne, stands the
seat of the archbishop surrounded by a circle of
enormous jasper columns, with colossal statues of
alabaster resting on the architraves; on either side
rise enormous bronze pulpits provided with two
great missals, and two gigantic organs, one in front

of the other, from which it seems that at any moment a flood of melody may burst forth and make the vault tremble.

The pleasure of one's admiration in these great cathedrals is almost always disturbed by importunate guides, who wish at any cost to amuse you after their fashion. And it was my misfortune to become convinced that the Spanish guides are the most persistent of their kind. When one of them has gotten it into his head that you are to spend the day with him, it is all over. You may shrug your shoulders, refuse to notice him, let him talk himself hoarse without so much as turning to look at him, wander about on your own account as though you had not seen him: it is all the same thing. In a moment of enthusiasm before some painting or statue a word escapes you, a gesture, a smile: it is enough. You are caught, you are his, you are the prey of this implacable human cuttle-fish, who, like the cuttle-fish of Victor Hugo, does not leave his victim until he has cut off his head. While I stood contemplating the statuary of the choir I saw one of these cuttle-fish out of the corner of my eye—a miserable old rake, who approached me with slow steps sidewise, like a cutthroat with the air of one who was saying, "Now I have got you!" I continued to look at the statues; the old man came up to my side, and he too began to look; then he suddenly asked me, "Do you wish my company?"

"No," I replied, "I don't need you."

And he continued, without any embarrassment,

"Do you know who Elpidius was?"

The question was so remarkable that I could not keep from asking in my turn,

"Who was he?"

"Elpidius," he replied, "was the second bishop of Toledo."

"Well, what of him?"

"'What of him?' It was the bishop Elpidius who conceived the idea of consecrating the church to the Virgin, and that is the reason why the Virgin came to visit the church."

"Ah! how do you know that?"

"'How do you know it?' You see it."

"Do you mean to say that it has been seen?"

"I mean to say that it is still to be seen: have the goodness to come with me."

So saying, he started off, and I followed him, very curious to learn what this visible form of the descent of the Virgin might be. We stopped in front of a sort of chapel close to one of the great pilasters of the central nave. The guide pointed out a white stone set in the wall covered by an iron net, and with this inscription running around it:

"Quando la reina del cielo
Puso los pies en el suelo,
En esta piedra lôs puso."

" When the Queen of heaven
 Descended to the earth,
 Her feet rested on this stone."

" Then the Holy Virgin has actually placed her
feet on this stone?" I asked.

" On this very stone," he replied ; and, thrusting
a finger between the strands of the iron net, he
touched the stone, kissed his finger, made the sign
of the cross, and turned toward me as if to say,
" Now it is your turn."

" My turn ?" I replied.   " Oh, really, my friend,
I cannot do it."

" Why ?"

" Because I do not feel myself worthy to touch
that sacred stone."

The guide understood, and, looking hard at me
with a serious aspect, he asked, " You do not
believe ?"

I looked at a pilaster.   Then the old man made
a sign for me to follow, and started toward a corner
of the church, murmuring with an air of sadness,
" *Cadanno es dueño de su alma* " (Every man is
master of his soul).

A young priest who was standing near, and who
had divined the cause of his words, cast a piercing
glance at me, and went off in an opposite direction,
muttering I know not what.

The chapels correspond in style with that of the
church : almost all of them contain some fine monu-

ments. In the chapel of Santiago, behind the high altar, are two magnificent tombs of alabaster which contain the remains of the constable Alvaro de Luna and his wife; in the chapel of San Ildefonso, the tomb of the cardinal Gil Carrillo de Albornoz; in the chapel of the " New Kings," the tombs of Henry II., John II., and Henry III.; in the chapel of the sacristy, a stupendous group of statues and busts of marble, silver, ivory, and gold, and a collection of crosses and relics of inestimable value, the remains of Saint Leucadia and Saint Eugenia preserved in two silver caskets exquisitely chased.

The Chapel Mozarabe, which is under the tower of the church, and was erected to perpetuate the tradition of the primitive Christian rite, is probably the most worthy of attention. One of its walls is entirely covered with a fresco, in the Gothic style, representing a conflict between the Moors and the Toledans—marvellously preserved, even to the most delicate lines. It is a painting worth a volume of history. In it one sees the Toledo of those times with all its walls and its houses; the habiliments of the two armies; the arms, faces, everything portrayed with an admirable finish and an unspeakable harmony of color which answers perfectly to the vague and fantastic idea which one may have formed of those centuries and those races. Two other frescoes on either side of the first represent the fleet which bore the Arabs into Spain, and they offer a thousand minute details of the mediæval marine and the very air of those times, if one may so speak, which makes one think of and see a thousand things not represented in the painting, as one hears distant music on looking at a landscape.

After the chapels one goes to see the sacristy, where are gathered enough riches to restore the finances of Spain to a sound basis. There is, among others, a vast room on the ceiling of which one sees a fresco by Luca Giordano, which represents a vision of paradise, with a myriad of angels, saints, and allegorical figures floating in the air or standing out like statues from the cornices of the walls in a thousand bold attitudes, with so much action and foreshortening that one is bewildered. The guide, pointing out this miracle of imagination and genius, which in the estimation of all artists, to use a very curious Spanish expression, is a work of *merito atroz* (of atrocious merit),—the guide bids you to look attentively at the ray of light which falls upon the walls from the centre of the vaulted ceiling. You look at it and then make a circuit of the room, and wherever you find yourself that ray of light is falling directly upon your head.

From this hall you pass into a room which is also beautifully painted in fresco by the nephew of Berruguete, and from it into a third, where a sacristan lays the treasures of the cathedral before your eyes—the enormous silver candlesticks; the pyxes flashing with rubies; the golden stands for the elevation of the Host, studded with diamonds; the damask vestments, embroidered in gold; the robes of the Virgin, covered with arabesques, garlands of flowers, and stars of pearl, which at every motion of the cloth flash forth in a thousand rays and colors and quite dazzle one's eyes. A hour is scarcely sufficient to see hurriedly all that display of treasures, which would certainly satisfy the ambition of ten queens and enrich the altars of ten cathedrals; and when, after he has shown you everything, the sacristan looks in your eyes for an expression of surprise, he finds only astonishment and stupefaction, which give evidence of an imagination wandering in far distant regions—in the realms of the Arabian legends where the kindly genii gather all the riches dreamed of by the glowing fancy of enamored sultans.

It was the eve of *Corpus Domini,* and in the sacristy they were preparing the robes for the processional. Nothing can be more unpleasant or more at variance with the quiet and noble sadness of the church than the theatrical hurry-scurry which one sees on such occasions. It is like being behind the scenes on the evening of a dress rehersal. From one room of the sacristy to another half-dressed boys were coming and going with a great clatter, carrying armfuls of surplices, stoles, and capes; here a sour-tempered sacristan was opening and banging the

doors of a wardrobe; there a priest, all red in the
face, was calling angrily to a chorister who did not
hear him; yonder other priests were running through
the room with their robes partly on their backs and
partly trailing behind them; some laughing, some
screaming, and some shouting from one room to
another at the top of their voices; everywhere one
heard a swish of skirts, a breathless panting, and an
indescribable stamping and tramping.

I went to see the cloister, but, as the door was
open through which one reaches it from the church,
I saw it before entering. From the middle of the
church one gets a glimpse of a part of the cloister-
garden, a group of fine leafy trees, a little grove, a
mass of luxuriant plants which seem to close the
doorway and look as though they are framed beneath
a graceful arch and between the two slender columns
of the portico which extends all around. It is a
beautiful sight, which makes one think of Oriental
gardens encircled by the columns of a mosque. The
cloister, which is very large, is surrounded by a colonnade, graceful, though severe in form; the walls
covered with great frescoes. The guide advised me
to rest here a little while before ascending to the
campanile. I leaned against a low wall in the shade
of a tree, and remained there until I felt able to
make another expedition, as the expression is.
Meanwhile, my commander extolled in bombastic
language the glories of Toledo, carrying his impu-

dence so far, in his patriotism, as to call it "a great commercial city" which could buy and sell Barcelona and Valencia, and a city strong enough, if need be, to withstand ten German armies and a thousand bat-teries of Krupp guns. After each of his exaggera-tions I kept spurring him on, and the good man en-joyed himself to the full. What pleasure there is in knowing how to make others talk! Finally, when the proud Toledan was so swollen with glory that the cloister could no longer hold him, he said to me, "We may go now," and led the way toward the door of the campanile.

When we were halfway up we stopped to take breath. The guide knocked at a little door, and out came a swaggering little sacristan, who opened another door, and made me enter a corridor where I saw a collection of gigantic puppets in very strange attire. Four of them, the guide told me, represented Europe, Asia, America, and Africa, and two others Faith and Religion; and they were so made that a man could hide in them and raise them from the ground.

"They take them out on the occasions of the royal fêtes," the sacristan added, "and carry them around through the city;" and, to show me how it was done, he crept in under the robes of Asia. Then he led me to a corner where there was an enormous monster which when touched, I know not where, stretched out a very long neck and a horrible head and made a dreadful noise. But he could not tell me what this ugly creature signified, and so invited me instead to admire the marvellous imagination of the Spaniards, which creates so "many new things" to sell in all the known world. I admired, paid, and continued the ascent with my Toledan cuttle-fish. From the top of the tower one enjoys a splendid view—the city, the hills, the river, a vast horizon, and, below, the great mass of the cathedral, which seems like a mountain of granite. But there is another elevation, a short distance away, from which one sees everything to a better advantage, and consequently I remained in the campanile only a few moments, especially as at that hour the sun was shining very strongly, confusing all the colors of the city and country in a flood of light.

From the cathedral my guide led me to see the famous church of *San Juan de los Reyes,* situated on the banks of the Tagus. My mind is still confused when I think of the windings and turnings which we were obliged to make in order to reach it. It was mid-day, the streets were deserted; gradually, as we went farther from the centre of the city, the solitude became more depressing; not a door or window was open, not the slightest sound was heard. For a moment I suspected that the guide was in league with some assassin to entice me into an out-of-the-way place and rob me; he had a suspicious face, and then he kept glancing here and

there with a suspicious air, like one meditating a crime.

"Is it much farther?" I would ask from time to time, and he would always answer: "It is right here," and yet we never reached it.

At a certain point my uneasiness changed into fear: in a narrow, tortuous street a door opened; two bearded men came out, made a sign to the cuttle-fish, and fell in behind us. I thought it was all over with me. There was only one way of escape—to strike the guide, knock him down, jump over his body, and run. But which way? And on the other side there came into my mind the high praises which Thiers bestows on the "Spanish legs" in his *History of the War of Independence;* and I thought that flight would only prove an opportunity to plant a dagger in my back instead of my stomach, Alas! to die without seeing Andalusia! To die after taking so many notes, after giving so many tips—to die with pockets full of letters of introduction, with a purse fat with doubloons—to die with a passport covered with seals—to die by treachery! As God willed, the two bearded men disappeared at the first corner and I was saved. Then, overwhelmed by compunction for suspecting that the poor old man could be capable of a crime, I came over to his left side, offered him a cigar, said that Toledo was worth two Romes, and showed him a thousand courtesies. Finally we arrived at *San Juan de los Reyes.*

It is a church which seems like a royal palace:
the highest part is covered by a balcony surrounded
with a honeycombed and sculptured breastwork,
upon which rises a series of statues of kings, and
in the middle stands a graceful hexagonal cupola
which completes the beautiful harmony of the edifice. From the walls hang long iron chains which
were suspended there by the Christian prisoners
released at the conquest of Granada, and which,
together with the dark color of the stone, give the
church a severe and picturesque appearance. We
entered, passed through two or three large, bare
rooms, unpaved, cluttered with piles of dirt and
heaps of rubbish, climbed a staircase, and came out
upon a high gallery inside the church, which is one
of the most beautiful and noblest of the monuments
of Gothic architecture. It has a single great nave
divided into four vaults, whose arches intersect
under rich rosettes. The pilasters are covered with
festoons and arabesques; the walls ornamented with
a profusion of bas-reliefs, with enormous shields
bearing the arms of Castile and Arragon, eagles,
dragons, heraldic animals, trailing vines, and emblem-
atic inscriptions; the gallery running all around the
room is perforated and carved with great elegance;
the choir is supported by a bold arch; the color of
the stone is light gray, and everything is admirably
finished and preserved, as if the church had been

built but a few years ago, instead of at the end of the fifteenth century.

From the church we descended to the cloister, which is, in truth, a miracle of architecture and sculpture. Graceful slender columns which could be broken in two by the stroke of a hammer, looking like the trunks of saplings, support capitals richly adorned like curving boughs; arches ornamented with flowers, birds, and grotesque animals in every sort of carving. The walls are covered with inscriptions in Gothic characters in a framework of leaves and very delicate arabesques. Wherever one looks one finds grace mingled with riches in enchanting harmony: it would not be possible to accumulate in an equal space and with more exquisite art a larger number of the most delicate and beautiful objects. It is a luxuriant garden of sculpture, a grand saloon embroidered, quilted, and brocaded in marble, a great monument, majestic as a temple, magnificent as a palace, delicate as a toy, and graceful as a flower.

After the cloisters one goes to see a picture-gallery which contains only some paintings of little value, and then to the convent with its long corridors, its narrow stairs, and empty cells, almost on the point of falling into ruins, and in some parts already in ruins; throughout bare and squalid like a building gutted by fire.

A little way from *San Juan de los Reyes* there is

another monument well worthy of attention, a curious record of the Judaic period—the synagogue
now known by the name of Santa Maria la Blanca.
One enters an untidy garden and knocks at the door
of a wretched-looking house. The door opens.
There is a delightful sense of surprise, a vision of
the Orient, a sudden revelation of another religion
and another world. There are five narrow alleys
divided by four long rows of little octagonal pilasters, which support as many Moorish arches with
stucco capitals of various forms; the ceiling is of
cedar-wood divided into squares, and here and there
on the walls are arabesques and Arabic inscriptions.
The light falls from above, and everything is white.
The synagogue was converted into a mosque by the
Arabs, and the mosque into a church by the Christians, so that, properly, it is none of the three,
although it still preserves the character of the
mosque, and the eye surveys it with delight, and
the imagination follows from arch to arch the fleeting images of a sensuous paradise.

When I had seen Santa Maria la Blanca, I had
not the strength to see anything else, and, refusing
all the tempting propositions of the guide, I told him
to lead me back to the hotel. After a long walk
through a labyrinth of narrow, deserted streets we
arrived there; I put a *peseta* and a half in the hand
of my innocent assassin, who found the fee too

small, and asked (how I laughed at the word!) for a little *gratificacion.*

I went into the dining-room to eat a chop or *chuleta* (which is pronounced *cuileta*), as the Spanish call it— a name at which they would turn up their noses in some of the provinces of Italy.

Toward evening I went to see the Alcazar. The name raises expectations of a Moorish palace, but there is nothing Moorish about it except the name. The building which one admires to-day was built in the reign of Charles V. on the ruins of a castle which was in existence as early as the eighth century, although the notices of it in contemporary chronicles are vague. This edifice rises upon a height over-looking the city, so that one sees its walls and towers from every point above the level of the streets, and the foreigner finds it a sure landmark amid the con-fusion and labyrinths of the city. I climbed the height by a broad winding street, like that one which runs from the plain up to the city, and found myself in front of the Alcazar. It is an immense square palace, at whose corners rise four great towers that give it the formidable appearance of a fortress. A vast square extends in front of the façade, and all around it runs a chain of embattled bulwarks of Oriental design. The entire building is of a decided chalky color, relieved by a thousand varied shades of that powerful painter of monu-ments, the burning sun of the South, and it appears even lighter against the very clear sky upon which the majestic form of the building is outlined.

The façade is carved in arabesques in a manner at once dignified and elegant. The interior of the palace corresponds with the exterior: it is a vast court surrounded by two orders of graceful arches, one above the other, supported by slender columns, with a monumental marble staircase starting at the centre of the side opposite the door, and a little way above the pavement divides into two parts that lead to the interior of the palace, the one on the right, the other on the left. To enjoy the beauty of the courtyard it is necessary to stand on the landing where the staircase separates: from that point one comprehends at a glance the complete harmony of the edifice, which inspires a sense of cheerfulness and pleasure, like fine music performed by hidden musicians.

Excepting the courtyard, the other parts of the building—the stairways, the rooms, the corridors—everything is in ruins or falling to ruins. They were at work turning the palace into a military school, whitewashing the walls, breaking down the partitions to make great dormitories, numbering the doors, and converting the palace into a barracks. Nevertheless, they left intact the great subterranean chambers which were used for stables at the time of Charles V., and which are still able to hold several thousand horses. The guide made me approach a

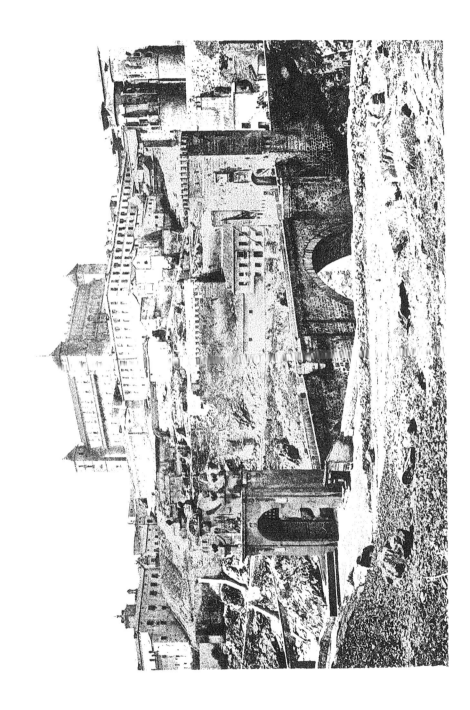

window from which I looked down into an abyss that gave me an idea of their vastness. Then we climbed a series of unsteady steps into one of the four towers; the guide opened with pincers and a hammer a window that had been nailed fast, and with the air of one who was announcing a miracle said to me, " Look, sir !"

It was a wonderful panorama. One had a bird's-eye view of the city of Toledo, street by street and house by house, as if one were looking at a map spread upon a table: here the cathedral, rising above the city like a measureless castle, and making all the buildings around it seem as small as toy houses; there the balcony of *San Juan de las Reyes*, crowned with statues; yonder the embattled towers of the New Gate, the circus, the Tagus running at the foot of the city between its rocky banks; and beyond the river, opposite the bridge of Alcantara, on a precipitous crag, the ruins of the ancient castle of San Servando; still farther off a verdant plain, and then rocks, hills, and mountains as far as the eye can see; and over all a very clear sky and the setting sun, which gilded the summits of the old buildings and flashed on the river like a great silver scarf.

While I was contemplating this magic spectacle the guide, who had read the *History of Toledo* and wished me to know the fact, was telling all sorts of stories with that manner, half poetical and half facetious, which is distinctive of the Spaniards of the South. Above all, he wished to explain the history of the work of fortification, and although, where he said that he saw clear and unmistakable remains which he pointed out to me, I saw nothing at all, I succeeded, nevertheless, in learning something about it.

He told me that Toledo had been thrice surrounded by a wall, and that the traces of all three walls were still clear. "Look!" he said; "follow the line which my finger indicates: that is the Roman wall, the innermost one, and its ruins are still visible. Now look a little farther on: that other one beyond it is the Gothic wall. Now let your glance describe a curve which embraces the first two: that is the Moorish wall, the most recent. But the Moors also built an inner wall on the ruins of the Roman wall: this you can easily see. Then observe the direction of the streets, which converge toward the highest point of the city; follow the line of the roofs—here, so; you will see that all the streets go up zigzag, and they were built purposely in this manner, so that the city could be defended even after the walls had been destroyed; and the houses were built so close one against another in order that it would be possible to jump from roof to roof, you see; and then the Arabs have left it in their writings. This is the reason that the Spanish gentlemen from Madrid make me laugh when they come here and say, 'Pooh! what streets!' You see, they do not know a particle of history : if they knew the least bit, if they read a little instead of spending their days on the Prado and in the Recoleto, they would understand that there is a reason for the narrow streets of Toledo, and that Toledo is not a city for ignoramuses."

I began to laugh.

"Do you not believe?" continued the custodian: "it is a sacred fact. Not a week ago, to cite a case, here comes a dandy from Madrid with his wife. Well, even as they were climbing the stairs they began to run down the city, the narrow streets, and the dark houses. When they came to this window and saw those two old towers down yonder on the plain on the left bank of the Tagus, they asked me what they were, and I answered, '*Los palacios de Galiana.*' 'Oh! what beautiful palaces!' they exclaimed, and began to laugh and looked in another direction. Why? Because they did not know their history. Now, I imagine that you do not know any better; but you are a stranger, and that makes a difference. Know, then, that the great emperor Charlemagne came to Toledo when he was a very young man. King Galafro was reigning then, and dwelt in that palace. King Galafro had a daughter Galiana, as beautiful as an angel; and, as Charlemagne was a guest of the king and saw the princess every day, he fell in love with her with all his heart, and so did the princess with him. But there was a rival between them, and this rival was the king of Guadalajara, a Moorish giant of herculean strength and the courage of a lion. This king, to see the princess without being seen, had a subterranean passage made all the way from the city of Guadalajara to the very foundation of the palace. But what good did it do? The princess could not even bear to see him, and as often as he came, so often did he return crestfallen; but not for this did the enamored king stop paying his court. And so much did he come hanging around that Charlemagne, who was not a man to be imposed upon, as you can imagine, lost his patience, and to end the matter challenged him. They fought: it was a terrible struggle, but the Moor, for all he was a giant, got the worst of it. When he was dead Charlemagne cut off his head and laid it at the feet of his love, who approved the delicacy of his offering, became a Christian, gave her hand to the prince, and went away with him to France, where she was proclaimed empress."

"And the head of the Moor?"

"You may laugh, but these are sacred facts. Do you see that old building down there at the highest point of the city? It is the church of San Ginés. And do you know what is inside of it? Nothing less than the door of an underground passage which extends three leagues beyond Toledo. You do not believe it? Listen! At the place where the church of San Ginés now stands there once was an enchanted palace before the Moors invaded Spain. No king had ever had the courage to enter it, and those who might possibly have been so bold did not do it because, according to the tradition, the first man who crossed that threshold would be the ruin of Spain. Finally King Roderic, before setting out for the battle of Guadalete, hoping to find in it some treasures which would furnish him means to resist the invasion of the Moors, had the doors broken open and entered, preceded by his warriors, who lighted the way. After a great deal of trouble to keep their torches lighted for the furious wind which came through the underground passages, they reached a mysterious room where they saw a chest which bore the inscription, 'He who opens me will see miracles.' The king commanded that it be opened: with incredible difficulty they succeeded in opening it, but, instead of gold or diamonds, they found only a roll of linen, on which were painted some armed Moors, with this inscription underneath: '*Spain will soon be destroyed by these.*' That very night a violent tempest arose, the enchanted palace fell, and a short time afterward the Moors entered Spain. You don't seem to believe it?"

"What stuff you are talking! How can I believe it?"

"But this history is connected with another.

You know, without doubt, that Count Julian, the commandant of the fortress of Ceuta, betrayed Spain and allowed the Moors to pass when he might have barred the way. But you do not know why Count Julian turned traitor. He had a daughter at Toledo, and this daughter went every day with a number of her young friends to bathe in the Tagus. As misfortune willed it, the place where they went to bathe, which was called *Los Baños de la Cava,* was near a tower in which King Roderic was accustomed to pass the mid-day hours. One day Count Julian's daughter, who was called Florinda, tired of sporting in the water, sat down on the river-bank and said to her companions, 'Companions, let us see who is the most beautiful.'—'Let us see!' they cried, and as soon done as said. They seated themselves around Florinda, and each one revealed her beauty. But Florinda surpassed them all, and, unfortunately, just at the moment when she said to the others, 'Look!' King Roderic put his head out of the window and saw them. Young and dissolute, you may imagine he took fire like a match, paid his court to the beautiful Florinda, ruined and abandoned her; and from this followed the fury of the revenge of Count Julian, the treason, and the invasion."

At this point it seemed that I had listened long enough: I gave the custodian two *reales,* which he took and put in his pocket with a dignified air, and, giving a last look at Toledo, I descended.

It was the hour for promenading. The principal
street, hardly wide enough for a carriage to pass
through, was full of people; there may have been a
few hundred persons, but they seemed like a great
crowd; it was dusk, the shops were closing, and a
few stray lights began to flicker here and there. I
went to get my dinner, but came out quickly, so as
not to lose sight of the promenade. It was night:
there was no other illumination save the moonlight,
and one could not see the faces of the people; I
seemed to be in the midst of a procession of spectres,
and was overwhelmed with sadness. "To think that
I am alone!" I said—"that in all this city there is
not a soul who knows me; that if I fall dead at this
moment, there would not be a dog to say, 'Poor
man! he was a good fellow!'" I saw joyous young
men pass, fathers of families with their children,
husbands or those who had the air of husbands
with beautiful creatures on their arms; every one
had a companion; they laughed and talked, and
passed without so much as looking at me. How
wretched I was! How happy I should have been if
a boy, a beggar, or a policeman had come up and
said, "It seems to me that I recognize you, sir"!—
"It is impossible, I am a foreigner, I have never
been in Toledo before; but it makes no matter;
don't go away; stay here, and we will talk a while,
for I am lonely."

In a happy moment I remembered that at Madrid

I had received a letter of introduction to a Toledan gentleman. I hurried to the hotel, took out my letter, and was at once shown to his house. The gentleman was at home and received me courteously. It was such a pleasure to hear my own name again that I could have thrown my arms around his neck. He was Antonio Gamero, the author of a highly esteemed *History of Toledo.* We spent the evening together. I asked him a hundred things; he told me a thousand, and read me some splendid passages from his book, which made me better acquainted with Toledo than I should otherwise have been in a month's residence there.

The city is poor, and worse than poor : it is dead ; the rich have abandoned it for Madrid ; the men of genius have followed the rich ; it has no commerce ; the manufacture of cutlery, the only industry which flourishes, provides a livelihood for some hundreds of families, but not for the city ; popular education is neglected ; the people are lazy and miserable.

But they have not lost their ancient character of nobility. Like all the peoples of great declining cities, they are proud and chivalrous ; they abhor baseness, deal justice with their own hands, when they can, to assassins and thieves and murderers ; and, although the poet Zorilla, in one of his ballads, has bluntly called them a silly people, they are not so ; they are alert and bold. They combine the seriousness of the Spaniards of the North with the vivacity of the

Spaniards of the South; they hold the middle ground
between the Castilian and the Andalusian; they
speak the language with refinement, with a greater
variety of inflexion than the people of Madrid, and
with greater precision than the people of Cordova
and Seville; they love poetry and music; they are
proud to number among their great men the gentle
Garcilaso de la Vega, the reformer of Spanish poetry,
and the illustrious Francisco de Rojas, the author of
the *Garcia del Castañar;* and they take pride in
welcoming within their walls artists and students
from all the countries in the world who come to
study the history of three nations and the monuments of three civilizations. But, whatever its
people may be, Toledo is dead; the city of Wamba,
of Alfonso the Brave, and of Padilla is nothing but
a tomb. Since Philip II. took from it the crown of
the capital, it has been steadily declining, and is still
declining, and it is consuming itself little by little,
solitary on the summit of its gloomy mountain, like
a skeleton abandoned on a rock in the midst of the
waves of the sea.

I returned to the hotel shortly before midnight.
Although the moon was shining brightly—for on
moonlight nights they do not illuminate the streets,
although the light of that silvery orb does not penetrate those narrow ways—I was obliged to grope my
way along like a thief. With my head full, as it
was, of fantastic ballads which describe the streets

of Toledo traversed at night by cavaliers muffled in their cloaks, singing under the windows of their ladies, fighting and killing one another, climbing into palaces and stealing the maidens away, I imagined I should hear the tinkle of guitars, the clashing of swords, and the cries of the dying. Nothing of the kind: the streets were deserted and silent and the windows dark, and one heard faintly from time to time at the corners and crossways the light step of some one passing or a fugitive whisper, the source of which one could in no way discover. I reached the hotel without harming any fair Toledan, which might have caused me some annoyance, and also without having any holes made in my stomach, which was undoubtedly a consolation.

The morning of the next day I visited the beautiful building of the hospital of San Cruz, the church of *Nuestra Señora del Transito,* an ancient synagogue, the ruins of an amphitheatre and of an arena where naval battles were fought in Roman times, and the famous manufactory of arms, where I bought a beautiful dagger with a silver handle and a blade covered with arabesques, which at this moment lies on my table, and when I shut my eyes and take it in my hand I seem to be still there, in the courtyard of the factory, a mile out of Toledo, under the midday sun, surrounded by a group of soldiers, and enveloped in a cloud of smoke from their cigarettes. I remember that as I was walking back to Toledo, as I was crossing a bit of country solitary as a desert and silent as the Catacombs, a terrible voice cried out, "Away with the foreigner!"

The voice came from the city. I stopped—I was the foreigner, that cry was directed at me, and my blood curdled; the solitude and silence of the place increased my fear. I started forward and the voice cried again, "Away with the foreigner!"

"Is it a dream?" I exclaimed, stopping again, "or am I awake? Who is shouting? Where is he? Why does he do it?"

I started on again, and the voice came the third time, "Away with the foreigner!"

I stopped the third time, and when, all disturbed, I cast my eyes around, I saw a boy sitting on the ground, who looked at me with a laugh and said, "He is a crazy man, who thinks he is living in the time of the War of Independence. Look, sir! that is the insane asylum." And he pointed out the place on a hill among the outermost houses of Toledo. I drew a long breath which would have blown out a torch.

In the evening I left Toledo, regretting that I had not time to see once and again all that was ancient and wonderful in it: this regret was tempered, however, by my ardent desire for Andalusia, which had not allowed me a moment's peace. But how long I saw Toledo before my eyes! How long I remembered and dreamed of those headlong rocks, those enormous walls, those dark streets, that fantastic appearance of a mediæval city! Even to-day I review the picture with a sort of sombre pleasure and grave melancholy, and with this picture before me my mind wanders back in a thousand strange thoughts among distant times and marvellous events.

CORDOVA.

CORDOVA.

On arriving at Castillejo I was obliged to wait until midnight for the Andalusia train. I dined on hard-boiled eggs and oranges, with a little sprinkling of Val de Peñas, murmured a poem of Espronceda, chatted a little with a custom-house officer who between parentheses made me a confession of his political faith—Amadeus, liberty, an increase of wages to the custom-house officers, etc; finally I heard the long-desired whistle, entered a railway-carriage crowded full of women, children, civil guards, boxes, cushions, and wraps, and away with a speed unusual for the Spanish railways. It was a beautiful night; my travelling-companions talked of bulls and Carlists; a beautiful girl, whom more than one devoured with his eyes, pretended to sleep that she might still further heighten their curiosity; some were rolling cigarettes, some peeling oranges, others humming songs from the *Zarzuella*. Nevertheless, I fell asleep in a few minutes. I believe I had already dreamed of the mosque of Cordova and the Alcazar of Seville, when I was aroused by a hoarse cry, "Daggers!"

"Daggers? Heavens! for whom?" Before I dis-

covered who had shouted there flashed before my
eyes a long sharp blade, and the unknown voice
asked again,

" Do you like it ?"

One must admit that there are pleasanter ways to
be awakened. I looked in the faces of my travelling-companions with an expression of consternation,
which made them all burst into a shout of laughter.
Then they explained that at every railway-station
there are vendors of knives and daggers who offer
tourists their wares, just as the boys offer newspapers
and refreshments in our country. Assured that my
life was safe, I bought my scarecrow—five francs ;
a splendid dagger for a villain in a tragedy, with an
ornamented handle, inscriptions on the blade, and a
sheath of embroidered velvet; and I put it in my
pocket, thinking that I might find it useful in Italy
to settle difficulties with my publishers.

The vendor must have had fifty of those knives
in a great red sash tied around his waist. Other
travellers bought them, the civil guards compli-
mented one of my neighbors on the good selection
he had made; the boys cried, " Buy me one too !"
The mammas answered, " We will buy you a bigger
one some other time." " O happy Spain !" I exclaimed, and thought with horror of our barbarous
laws, which forbid the innocent amusement of a little
cold steel.

We crossed La Mancha, the celebrated La Mancha,

the immortal theatre of the adventures of Don
Quixote. It is such a place as I imagined—wide,
bare plains, long tracts of sandy soil, here and there
a windmill, a few wretched villages, lonely lanes,
and forsaken huts. On seeing these places I felt
that vague sense of melancholy which steals over
me as I read the book of Cervantes, and repeated to
myself what I always say on reading it: "This man
cannot make one laugh without also making one's
tears flow as the laughter dies away."

Don Quixote is a sad and sombre figure: his madness is a lament; his life is the history of the dreams,
illusions, awakenings, and aberrations of each of us;
the struggle of reason with imagination, of truth
with falshood, of the ideal with the real. We all
have something of Don Quixote in our nature; we
all mistake windmills for giants; we are all now and
then spurred on by the impulse of enthusiasm, only
to be driven back by the laugh of scorn; we are
each a mixture of the sublime and the ridiculous;
we all feel bitterly and profoundly the eternal conflict between the grandeur of our aspirations and the
impotence of our powers. O beautiful dreams of
childhood and youth! Generous impulses to con-
secrate our life to the defence of virtue and justice,
fond imaginations of dangers faced, of adventurous
struggles, of magnanimous deeds, and sublime loves,
fallen one by one, like the petals of a flower, in the
narrow and uneventful paths of life! To what new

life have they arisen in our soul, and what vague thoughts and profound inspirations have we derived from thee, O generous and hapless cavalier of the sad figure!

We arrived at Argamasilla de Alba, where Don Quixote was born and died, and where poor Cervantes, the tax-gatherer of the great priory of San Juan, was arrested by angry debtors and imprisoned in a house which is said to be still in existence, and where he probably conceived the plan of his romance. We passed near the village of Val de Peñas, which gives its name to one of the most exquisite wines of Spain—dark, tingling, exhilarating, the only one, forsooth, which permits the foreigner from the North to indulge in copious libations at his meals; and finally we arrived at Santa Cruz de Mudela, a village famous for its manufactories of *navajas* (knives and razors), near which the way begins to slope gently upward toward the mountain.

The sun had risen, the women and children had left the carriage, and a number of peasants, officers, and *toreros* had entered on their way to Seville. One saw in that small space a variety of costume which would not be seen even in an Italian marketplace—the pointed caps of the peasants of the Sierra Morena, the red trousers of the soldiers, the great sombreros of the *picadores*, the shawls of the gypsies, the mantles of the Catalans, Toledo blades hanging from the walls, capes, belts, and finery of all the colors of a harlequin.

The train entered the rocks of the Sierra Morena, which separate the valley of the Guadiana from that of the Guadalquivir, famous for the songs of poets and the deeds of brigands. The railway runs at times between two walls of rock sheer from the very peaks, so high that to see the top one must put one's head all the way out of the window and turn one's face up, as if to look at the roof of the carriage. Sometimes the rocks are farther away and rise one above the other, the first like enormous broken stones, the last straight and sharp like bold towers rising upon measureless bastions; between them a mass of boulders cut into teeth, steps, crests, and humps, some almost hanging in the air, others separated by deep caverns and frightful precipices, presenting a confusion of curious forms, of fantastic suggestions of houses, gigantic figures and ruins, and offering at every step a thousand outlines and surprising appearances; and, together with this infinite variety of form, an infinite variety of color, shadow, dancing and changing light. For long distances, to the right, to the left, and overhead, one sees nothing but stone, without a house, a path, or a patch of ground where a man could set his foot, and, as one advances, rocks, ravines, and precipices: everything grows larger, deeper, and higher until one reaches the summit of the Sierra, where the solemn majesty of the spectacle provokes a cry of wonder.

The train stopped a few minutes, and all the travellers put their heads out of the window.

"Here," said one in a loud voice,—"here Cardenio jumped from rock to rock to do penance for his sins" (Cardenio, one of the most remarkable characters in *Don Quixote*, who jumped about among the rocks of the Sierra in his shirt to do penance for his sins). "I wish," continued the traveller, "that Sagasta might have to do the same."

They all laughed, and began to find, each one on his own account, some political enemy upon whom in imagination he might inflict this punishment: one proposed Serrano, another Topete, and a third another, and so on, until in a few minutes, if their desires had been realized, one might have seen the entire Sierra filled with ministers, generals, and deputies in their shirts skipping from crag to crag like the famous rock of Alessandro Manzoni.

The train started, the rocks disappeared, and the delightful valley of the Guadalquivir, the garden of Spain, the Eden of the Arabs, the paradise of painters and of poets, blessed Andalusia, revealed herself to my eyes. I can still feel the thrill of childish joy with which I hurried to the window, saying to myself, "Let me enjoy it."

For a long distance the country does not offer any new appearance to the ardent curiosity of the travel-

ler. At Vilches there is a vast plain, and beyond it
the level country of Tolosa, where Alfonso VIII.,
king of Castile, won the celebrated victory of *de las
Navas* over the Mussulman army. The sky was as
clear as air—in the distance rose the mountains of
the Sierra de Segura. Suddenly I made one of
those quick motions which seemed to correspond to
an unuttered cry of astonishment: the first aloes
with their broad heavy leaves, the unexpected har-
bingers of the tropical vegetation, rise beside the
road. Beyond them the fields sprinkled with flowers
begin to appear. The first fields sprinkled, those
which follow almost covered, then vast tracts of
country wholly clothed, with wild poppies, daisies,
iris, mushrooms, cowslips, and buttercups, so that
the country appears like a succession of vast carpets
of purple and gold and snowy white, and far away,
among the trees, innumerable streaks of blue, white,
and yellow until the eye is lost; and hard by, on the
edge of the ditches, the mounds, and the banks, even
to the very track, flowers in beds, groups, and clusters, one above the other, fashioned like great
bouquets, trembling on their stems, which one can
almost touch with the hand. Then waving fields of
grain with great heavy bearded heads, bordered by
long gardens of roses; then orange-orchards and
vast olive-groves; hillocks varied by a hundred
shades of green, surmounted by ancient Moorish
towers, dotted with many-colored cottages, with here

and there white, graceful bridges, which span rivulets hidden by the trees. On the horizon rise the snowy peaks of the Sierra Nevada, and below this white line other blue undulating lines of the nearer mountains. The country grows ever more various and blooming: Arjonilla, embowered in an orange-grove whose limits are lost in the distance; Pedro Abad, in the midst of a plain covered with vineyards and orchards; Ventas de Alcolea, on the hills of the Sierra Morena, crowned with villas and gardens. We are drawing near to Cordova: the train flies; one sees little stations half hidden among trees and flowers; the wind blows the rose-leaves into the cars, great butterflies sail past the windows, a delicious perfume fills the air, the travellers are singing, we pass through an enchanted garden, the aloes, oranges, palms, and villas become more frequent; one hears a cry: "Here is Cordova!"

How many beautiful images and how many memories are recalled by that name!

Cordova, the ancient pearl of the Occident, as the Moorish poets called her, the city of cities, Cordova of the thirty burgs and the three thousand mosques, which contained within her walls the greatest temple of Islam! Her fame spread through the Orient and obscured the glory of ancient Damascus,—from the remotest regions of Asia the faithful journeyed toward the banks of the Guadalquivir to prostrate themselves in the marvellous mihrab of her mosque,

in the blaze of a thousand brazen lamps cast from
the bells of the Spanish cathedrals. From every
part of the Mohammedan world artists, scholars, and
poets crowded to her flourishing schools, her vast
libraries, and the magnificent courts of her caliphs.
Hither flowed wealth and beauty, drawn by the
fame of her splendor.

And from here they separated, eager for knowledge,
along the coasts of Africa, among the schools of Tu-
nis, Cairo, Bagdad, and Cufa, as far as India and
China, in search of books, inspiration, and memories; and the poems sung on the slopes of the Sierra
Morena flew from harp to harp even to the valleys
of the Caucasus, to make the hearts of pilgrims burn
within them. The beautiful, the mighty, the wise
Cordova, crowned with three thousand villages,
proudly reared her white minarets among her orange-groves and spread through the divine valley a
voluptuous air of gladness and glory.

I descend from the train, cross a garden, and look
around: I am alone; the travellers who came with
me have disappeared in different directions; I still
hear the rumble of the receding carriages; then all is
silent.

It is mid-day: the sky is very clear, the air burning. I see two white cottages; it is the opening of
a street; I enter and go forward. The street is narrow, the houses small as the little villas built on the
hillocks of artificial gardens; nearly all of them are

one story in height, with windows a little way from the ground, roofs so low that one can almost touch them with a cane, and very white walls. The street makes a turn; I look down it; no one is in sight; I do not hear a step nor a voice. "It must be an abandoned street," I say, and turn in another direction: white cottages, closed windows, solitude, and silence. "Where am I?" I ask myself.

I walk on: the street is so narrow and crooked that a carriage could not pass through it; to the right and left one sees other deserted streets, other white houses, and other closed windows; my step echoes as in a corridor; the white of the walls is so bright that the reflection almost blinds me, and I am obliged to walk with my eyes closed; I seem to be passing through snow. I reach a little square: everything is closed, there is no one about. Then a feeling of vague melancholy begins to steal into my heart, such as I have never felt before, a mingling of enjoyment and sorrow like that which children experience when after a long run they find themselves in a beautiful country-place and enjoy it, but with a tremor of fear at being so far away from home. Above the many roofs rise the palms of the inner gardens. O fantastic legends of odalisques and caliphs!

On from street to street and square to square; I meet a few persons, but they all pass and disappear like phantoms. The streets are all alike, the houses

have only two or four windows; and there is not a
stain, not a scratch, not a crack in the walls, which
are as smooth and white as a sheet of paper. Now
and then I hear a whisper behind a venetian blind,
and almost at the same moment see a dark head with
a flower in the hair peep out and disappear. I approach a door.

A *patio!* How shall I describe a *patio?* It is not
a courtyard, it is not a garden, it is not a room; it is
the three in one. Between the *patio* and the street
there is a vestibule. On the four sides of the *patio*
rise graceful columns which support a sort of balcony enclosed in glass at the height of the second
story; over the balcony extends a canvas which
shades the court. The vestibule is flagged with
marble, the doorway supported by columns surmounted by bas-reliefs and closed by a delicate iron
lattice of very beautiful design. At the back of the
patio, opposite the doorway, stands a statue, in the
centre a fountain, and all around chairs, work-tables,
paintings, and vases of flowers. I run to another
door. Another *patio*, its walls covered with ivy,
and a line of niches containing statuettes and urns.
I hurry to a third door. A *patio* with its walls
adorned with mosaic, a palm in the centre, and all
around a mass of flowers. A fourth door. Behind
the *patio* another vestibule, and then a second *patio*,
in which one sees other statues, columns, and fountains. And all these rooms and gardens are clean

and tidy, so that you could pass your hands over the walls and along the floor without leaving a mark; and they are fresh and fragrant, lighted with a dim light which heightens their beauty and mystery.

Still forward, from street to street, at random. Gradually, as I walk on, my curiosity increases and I hasten my steps. It seems impossible that the whole city can be like this: I am afraid of coming upon a house or finding a street which will remind me of other cities and rouse me from my pleasant dream.

But, no: the dream is unbroken. Everything is small, graceful, mysterious. Every hundred paces a deserted little square, in which I stop breathless; now and then a crossway, and not a living soul; and everything always white—closed windows and silence. At every door there is a new spectacle: arches, columns, flowers, fountains, palms; a marvellous variety of design, color, light, perfume, here of roses, there of oranges, yonder of violets; and with the perfume a breath of fresh air, and borne on the air the subdued sound of women's voices, the rustling of leaves, and the singing of birds—a sweet and various harmony, which, without disturbing the silence of the street, soothes the ear like the echo of distant music. Ah! it is not a dream! Madrid, Italy, Europe, surely they are far, far away. Here one lives another life, here one breathes the air of another world; I am in the Orient.

I remember that at a certain point I stopped in the middle of the street and suddenly discovered, I know not how, that I was sad and restless, and that in my heart there was a void which neither admiration nor enjoyment could fill. I felt an irrepressible necessity of entering those houses and those gardens, of tearing asunder, so to speak, the mysterious veil which concealed the life of the unknown people within; of sharing in that life; of grasping some hand and gazing into two pitying eyes, and saying, "I am a stranger, I am alone; I too want to be happy; let me linger among your flowers, let me enjoy all the secrets of your paradise, teach me who you are and how you live; smile on me and calm me, for my head is burning!"

And this sadness grew upon me until I said to myself, "I cannot stay in this city; I am suffering here; I will leave it!"

And I believe I should have left if at a happy moment I had not remembered that I carried in my pocket a letter of introduction to two young men of Cordova, brothers of a friend of mine in Florence. I dismissed the idea of leaving, and started at once to find them.

How they laughed when I told them of the impression Cordova had made upon me! They proposed that we go at once to see the cathedral; so we turned down a narrow white street and were off.

The mosque of Cordova, which was converted into a cathedral after the overthrow of the Moors, but which must always remain a mosque, was built on the ruins of the original cathedral, a little way back from the bank of the Guadalquivir. Abdurrahman commenced its construction in the year 785 or 786 A. D. "Let us rear a mosque," said he, "which shall surpass that of Bagdad, of Damascus, and of Jerusalem—a mosque which shall be the greatest temple of Islam, one which shall become the Mecca of the West." They undertook the work with great ardor. Christian slaves carried the stone for its foundations from their ruined churches; Abdurrahman himself worked an hour every day; in a few years the mosque was built, the caliphs who succeeded Abdurrahman embellished it, and after a century of almost continuous labor it was finished.

"Here we are!" said one of my friends, stopping suddenly in front of a vast edifice.

I thought it was a fortress, but it was the wall which surrounds the mosque—an old embattled wall in which there were at one time twenty great bronze doors ornamented with the most beautiful arabesques, and arched windows supported by graceful columns, now covered by a triple coat of plaster. A turn around this wall is a nice little walk to take after dinner: one may judge, therefore, of the vast size of the building.

The principal door of the enclosure is north of

the point where rises the minaret of Abdurrahman,
f.om whose summit floated the Mohammedan stand-
ard. We entered: I expected to see at once the
interior of the mosque, but found myself in a garden
full of orange trees, cypresses, and palms, surrounded
on three sides by a very beautiful portico and closed
on the fourth side by the façade of the mosque.
In the midst of this garden there was, in the time
of the Moors, the fountain for their ablutions, and
in the shade of these trees the faithful refreshed
themselves before entering the sanctuary.

I stood for some moments looking around and
breathing in the fresh odorous air with the liveliest
sense of pleasure, and my heart leaped at the
thought of the famous mosque standing there before
me, and I felt myself impelled toward the door by
a boundless curiosity, and at the same time restrained
by I know not what feeling of childish hesitation.

" Let us enter," said my companions. " One
moment more," I replied: " let me thoroughly enjoy
the delight of anticipation." Finally I moved forward and ·entered, without so much as looking at
the marvellous doorway which my companions
pointed out.

What I did or said on entering I do not know, but
some strange exclamation must surely have escaped
me or I must have made an odd gesture, for some
persons who were just then coming toward me began
to laugh and turned again to look around, as if to

discover the reason of the profound emotion which
I had manifested.

Imagine a forest and suppose yourself in the
thickest part, where you see only the trunks of
trees. So in the mosque wherever you turn your
gaze is lost among the columns. It is a forest of
marble whose boundaries one cannot discover. One
follows with the eye, one by one, those lengthening
rows of columns crossed at every step by innumerable other rows, and perceives a dimly-lighted background in which one seems to see the gleaming of
still other columns. There are nineteen naves which
extend in the direction in which you enter, crossed
by thirty-three other naves, and supported, in all,
by more than nine hundred columns of porphyry,
jasper, onyx, and marble of every color. Each
column is surmounted by a pilaster, and between one
column and the next bends an arch, and a second
arch above the first extends from pilaster to pilaster,
both of them in the form of a horseshoe; and so,
imagining the columns to be the trunks of so many
trees and the arches to represent the branches, the
resemblance of the mosque to a forest is complete.

The central nave, much larger than the others,
leads to the Maksura, the most sacred part of the
temple, where they worshipped the Koran. Here
from the vaulted windows steals a faint ray of light
which glides along a row of columns; there a dark
place, and yonder another ray pierces the gloom of

another nave. It is impossible to express the feeling of mystical wonder which fills one's mind at this spectacle. It is like the sudden revelation of a religion, a nature, and a life unknown, leading the fancy captive among the delights of that paradise of love and pleasure where the blessed, sitting in the shade of leafy plane trees and of thornless roses, drink from crystal beakers wine gleaming like pearls, mixed by immortal children, and repose in the embrace of lovely virgins with great dark eyes! All the images of that external pleasure, eager, warm, and glowing, which the Koran promises to the faithful, crowd upon the mind at the first sight of the mosque, and give one a delicious moment of intoxication which leaves in the heart an indescribable feeling of gentle melancholy. A brief tumult in the mind and a rapid thrill which goes tingling through the veins,—such is one's first sensation on entering the cathedral of Cordova.

We began to wander from passage to passage, examining everything minutely. What a variety in that edifice which at first sight appears so uniform! The proportions of the columns, the design of the capitals, the form of the arches change, one may say, at every step. The greater part of the columns are old and were taken by the Moors from Northern Spain, Gaul, and Roman Africa, and one is said to have belonged to a temple of Janus, upon whose ruins stood the church which the Arabians destroyed to build the mosque. On several of the capitals one may still see the traces of the crosses carved upon them, which the Arabians broke off with their hammers. In some of the columns iron rings are fastened to which it is said the Arabians bound the Christians, and among the others there is one pointed out to which the popular tradition narrates a Christian was bound for many years, and in that time, by continually scratching with his nails, he succeeded in engraving a cross on the stone, which the guides show with profound veneration.

We entered the Maksura, which is the most perfect and marvellous work of Moorish art of the twelfth century. At the entrance there are three continuous chapels, with vaulted roofs formed by indented arches, and walls covered with magnificent mosaics which represent wreaths and flowers and passages from the Koran. At the back of the middle chapel is the principal *mihrab*, the holy place, where dwelt the Spirit of God. It is a niche with an octagonal base enclosed above by a colossal marble shell. In the *mihrab* was kept the Koran written by the hands of the caliph Othman, covered with gold, adorned with pearls, suspended above a seat of aloe-wood; and here came thousands of the faithful to make the circuit of it seven times on their knees. On approaching the wall I felt the pavement slipping from under me: the marble had been worn hollow!

On leaving the niche I stood a long time contemplating the vault and the walls of the principal chapel, the only part of the mosque which has been preserved almost intact. It is a dazzling flash of crystals of a thousand colors, an interweaving of arabesques which confuse the mind, a mingling of bas-reliefs, gilding, ornaments, and minute details of design and coloring of a delicacy, grace, and perfection which would prove the despair of the most patient artist. It is impossible to retain in one's mind any part of that prodigious work: you might return a hundred times to look at it, but in reality it would only remain before your eyes as a tantalizing blur of blue, red, green, golden, and luminous shades of colors, or a very intricate piece of embroidery continually and rapidly changing in color and design. Only from the ardent and tireless imagination of the Moors could such a miracle of art have issued.

We began to wander through the mosque again, observing here and there on the walls the arabesques of the ancient doorways which are now and then discovered under the detestable plaster of the Christians. My companions looked at me, laughed, and whispered something to each other. "Have you not seen it yet?" one of them asked me.

"What do you mean?"

They looked at me again and smiled.

"You think you have seen all the mosque, do you?" continued my companion.

"Yes, indeed," I replied, looking around.

"Well," said the first, "you have not seen it all, and what remains to be seen is nothing less than a church.

"A church?" I exclaimed stupefied, "but where is it?"

"Look!" answered my other companion, pointing; "it is in the very centre of the mosque."

"By the powers!' And I had nòt seen it!

From this one may judge of the vastness of the mosque.

We went to see the church. It is beautiful and very rich, with a magnificent high altar and a choir worthy to stand beside those in the cathedrals of Burgos and Toledo, but, like everything out of place, it moves one to anger rather than admiration. Without this church the appearance of the mosque would be much improved. Charles V., who himself gave the chapter permission to build it, repented when he saw the Mohammedan temple for the first time. Besides the church there is a sort of Moorish chapel in a good state of preservation, rich in mosaics not less varied and splendid than those of the Maksura, and where it is said the ministers of the faith used to assemble to discuss the book of the Prophet.

Such is the mosque to-day. But what must it have been in the time of the Arabs! It was not entirely enclosed by a wall, but open, so that one could see the garden from every side, and from the garden one could look to the very end of the long naves, and the fragrance of orange-blossoms and flowers was wafted even to the vaulted roofs of the Maksura. The columns, which now number less than a thousand, were then fourteen hundred in number; the ceiling was of cedar-wood and larch, carved and enamelled with exquisite workmanship; the walls were lined with marble; the light of eight hundred lamps filled with fragrant oil made the crystals in the mosaic-work flash like pearls, and produced on the pavement, the arches, and the walls a marvellous play of color and reflection. "A sea of splendors," sang a poet, filled the mysterious enclosure, and the warm air was laden with perfume and harmony, and the thoughts of the faithful wandered and were lost in the labyrinth of columns gleaming like lances in the sun.

Frederick Schrack, the author of a good work on the *Poetry and Art of the Moors in Spain and Sicily*, gives a description of the mosque on a day of solemn festival, which forms a very lively image of the Mohammedan religion and completes the picture of the monument.

On both sides of the almimbar, or pulpit, wave two banners, to signify that Islam has triumphed over Judaism and Christianity and that the Koran has conquered both the Old and the New Testament. The *almnedani* ascend to the gallery of the high minaret and intone the salam, or salutation, to the Prophet. Then the aisles of the mosque are filled with believers, who with white vestments and in festal attire come together to worship. In a few moments, throughout the length and breadth of the edifice, one sees only kneeling people. The caliph enters by the secret way which leads from the Alcazar to the temple, and seats himself in his elevated station. A reader of the Koran reads a *sura* from the low desk of the pulpit.

The voice of the muezzin sounds again, calling men to midday prayer. All the faithful rise and murmur their prayers, bowing as they do so. An attendant of the mosque opens the doors of the pulpit and seizes a sword, and, holding it, he turns toward Mecca, admonishing the people to worship Mohammed, while the *mubaliges* are chanting his praises from the gallery. Then the preacher mounts the pulpit, taking from the hand of the servant the sword, which calls to mind and symbolizes the subjection of Spain to the power of Islam. It is the day when the *Djihad*, or the holy war, must be proclaimed, the call for all able-bodied men to go to war and descend into the battle-field against the Christians. The multitude listens with silent devotion to the sermon, woven from texts of the Koran, which begins in this wise:

"Praise be to Allah, who has increased the glory of Islam, thanks to the sword of the champion of the faith, who in his holy book has promised succor and victory to the believer.

"Allah scatters his benefits over the world.

"If he did not put it in the hearts of men to take up arms against their fellows, the world would be lost.

"Allah has ordained to fight against the people until they know that there is but one God.

"The torch of war will not be extinguished until the end of the world.

"The blessing of God will fall upon the mane of the war-horse to the day of judgment.

"Armed from head to foot or but lightly clad, it matters not—up and away!

"O believers! what shall be done to you if, when called to the battle, you remain with face turned to the earth?

"Do you prefer the life of this world to the life to come?

"Believe me, the gates of paradise stand in the shadow of the sword.

"He who dies in battle for the cause of God shall wash away with his blood all the defilement of his sins.

"His body shall not be wasted like the other bodies of the dead, for on the day of judgment his wounds shall yield a fragrance like musk.

"When the warriors present themselves at the gates of paradise, a voice within shall ask, 'What have you done in your life?'

"And they shall answer, 'We have brandished the sword in the struggle for the cause of God.'

"Then the eternal doors will swing open, and the warriors will enter forty years before the rest.

"Up, then, ye faithful; leave your women, your children, your kindred, and your goods, and go out to the holy war!

"And thou, O God, Lord of this present world and of that which is to come, fight for the armies of those who recognize thy unity! Cast down the unbelievers, the idolaters, and the enemies of thy holy faith! Overwhelm their standards, and give them, with whatever they possess, as a prey to the Mussulman!"

The preacher as he ends his discourse turns toward the congregation and exclaims, "Ask of God!" and begins to pray in silence.

All the faithful, with heads bowed to the ground, follow his example. The *mubaliges* chant, "Amen! Amen, O Lord of all being!" Burning like the heat which precedes the oncoming tempest, the enthusiasm of the multitude, restrained at first in awful silence, now breaks out into deep murmurs, which rise like the waves and swell through all parts of the temple, until finally the naves, the chapels, and the vaulted roofs resound to the echo of a thousand voices united in a single cry: "There is no God but Allah!"

The mosque of Cordova is even to-day, by universal consent, the most beautiful temple of Islam and one of the most marvellous monuments in the world.

When we left the mosque it was already long past the hour of the siesta, which everybody takes in the cities of Southern Spain, and which is a necessity by reason of the insupportable heat of the noon hours. The streets began to fill with people. "Alas!" said I to my companions, "how badly the silk hat looks in the streets of Cordova! How have you the heart to introduce the fashion-plates in this beautiful Oriental picture? Why do you not adopt the dress of the Moors?" Coxcombs pass, work-men, and girls: I looked at them all with great curiosity, hoping to find one of those fantastic figures which Doré has represented as examples of the Andalusian type, with that dark-brown com-plexion, those thick lips, and large eyes, but I saw none. Walking toward the centre of the city, I saw the first Andalusian women—ladies, girls and women of the middle classes—almost all small, grace-ful, and well-formed, some of them beautiful, many attractive in appearance, but the greater part neither one thing nor the other, as is the case in all coun-tries. In their dress, with the exception of the so-called mantilla, they do not differ at all from the French women nor from those of our country—great masses of false hair in plaits, knots, and long curls, short petticoats, long plaited over-skirts, and boots with heels as sharp as daggers. The ancient Andalusian costume has disappeared from the city.

I thought that in the evening the streets would be crowded, but I saw only a few people, and only in the streets of the principal quarters; the others remain as empty as at the hour of the siesta. And one must pass through those deserted streets at night to enjoy Cordova. One sees the light streaming from the *patios;* one sees in the dark corners fond lovers in close colloquy, the girls usually at the windows, with a hand resting lightly on the iron grating, and the young men close to the wall in poetic attitudes, with watchful eyes, but not so watchful, however, as to make them take their lips from those hands before they discover that some one is passing; and one hears the sound of guitars, the murmur of fountains, sighs, the laughter of children, and mysterious rustlings.

The following morning, still stirred by the Oriental dreams of the night, I again began my wandering through the city. To describe all that is remarkable there one would require a volume: it is a very museum of Roman and Arabian antiquities, and one finds a profusion of martial columns and inscriptions in honor of the emperors; the remains of statues and bas-reliefs; six ancient gates; a great bridge over the Guadalquivir dating from the time of Octavius Augustus and restored by the Arabians; ruins of towers and walls; houses which belonged

to the caliphs, and which still contain the columns
and the subterranean arches of the bathing apartments; and everywhere there are doors, vestibules,
and stairways that would delight a legion of archæ-
ologists.

Toward noon, as I was passing through a lonely
little street, I saw a sign on the wall of a house
beside a Roman inscription, *Casa de huespedes.*
Almuerzos y comidas, and as I read I felt the gnaw-
ing, as Giusti says, of such a desperate hunger that
I determined to give it a quietus in this little shop
upon which I had stumbled. I passed through a
little vestibule, and found myself in a *patio.* It was
a poor little *patio,* without marble floor and without
fountains, but white as snow and fresh as a garden.
As I saw neither tables nor chairs, I feared I had
mistaken the door and started to go out. A little
old woman bustled out from I know not where and
stopped me.

"Have you anything to eat?" I demanded.

"Yes, sir," she answered.

"What have you?"

"Eggs, sausages, chops, peaches, oranges, and
wine of Malaga."

"Very good: you may bring everything you
have."

She commenced by bringing me a table and a
chair, and I sat down and waited. Suddenly I heard
a door open behind me and turned. . . . Angels of

heaven! what a sight I saw!—the most beautiful of all the most beautiful Andalusians, not only of those whom I saw at Cordova, but of all those whom I afterward saw at Seville, Cadiz, and Granada: if I may be allowed to use the word, a superb girl, who would make one flee or commit some deviltry; one of those faces which make you cry, "O poor me!" like Giuseppe Baretti when he was travelling in Spain. For some moments she stood motionless with her eyes fixed on mine as if to say, "Admire me;" then she turned toward the kitchen and cried, "*Tia, despachate!*" ("Hurry up, aunty!") This gave me an opportunity of thanking her with a stammering tongue, and gave her a pretence for approaching me and replying, "It is nothing," with a voice so gentle that I was obliged to offer her a chair, whereupon she sat down. She was a girl about twenty years old, tall, straight as a palm, and dark, with two great eyes full of sweetness, lustrous and humid as though she had just been in tears: she wore a mass of wavy jet-black hair with a rose among her locks. She seemed like one of the Arabian virgins of the tribe of the Usras for whom men died of love.

She herself opened the conversation:

"You are a foreigner, I should think, sir?"

"Yes."

"French?"

"Italian."

"Italian ?   A fellow-countryman of the king ?"

" Yes."

" Do you know him, sir ?"

" By sight !"

" They say he is a handsome young fellow."

I did not answer, and she began to laugh, and asked me, " What are you looking at, sir ?" and, still laughing, she hid her foot, which on taking her seat she thrust well forward that I might see it. Ah! there is not a woman in that country who does not know that the feet of the Andalusians are famous throughout the world.

I seized the opportunity of turning the conversation upon the fame of the Andalusian women, and expressed my admiration in the most fervent words of my vocabulary.   She allowed me to talk on, looking with great attention at the crack in the table, then raising her face, she asked me, " And in Italy, how are the women there ?"

" Oh, there are beautiful women in Italy too."

" But . . . they are cold ?"

" Oh no, not at all," I hastened to respond ; " but, you know, . . . in every country the women have an *I-know-not-what* which distinguishes them from the women of all other countries ; and among them all the *I-know-not-what* of the Andalusians is probably the most dangerous for a poor traveller whose hairs have not turned gray.   There is a word to express what I mean : if I could remember it, I would say it to you; I would say, "*Señorita,* you are the most . . ."

"*Salada,*" exclaimed the girl, covering her face with her hands.

"*Salada!* . . . the most *salada* Andalusian in Cordova."

Salada is the word commonly used in Andalusia to describe a woman beautiful, charming, affectionate, languid, ardent, what you will—a woman with two lips which say, "Drink me," and two eyes which make one close one's teeth.

The aunt brought me the eggs, chops, sausage, and oranges, and the girl continued the conversation: "Sir, you are an Italian: have you seen the Pope?"

"No, I am sorry to say."

"Is it possible? An Italian who has not seen the Pope! And tell me, sir: why do the Italians make him suffer so much?"

"Suffer in what way?"

"Yes. They say that they have shut him up in his house and thrown stones at the windows."

"Oh no! Don't believe it! There is not a partiele of truth in it," etc., etc.

"Have you seen Venice, sir?"

"Venice? oh yes."

"Is it true that it is a city which floats on the sea?"

And here she made a thousand requests that I

would describe Venice, and that I would tell her
what the people were like in that strange city, and
what they do all the day long, and how they dress.
And while I was talking—besides the pains I took
to express myself with a little grace, and to eat
meanwhile the badly-cooked eggs and stale sausage
—I was obliged to see her draw nearer and nearer
to me, that she might hear me better perhaps, without being conscious of the act. She came so close
that I could smell the fragrance of the rose in her
hair and feel her warm breath; I was obliged, I may
say, to make three efforts at once—one with my
head, another with my stomach, and a third with
both—especially when, now and then, she would say,
" How beautiful !"—a compliment which applied to
the Grand Canal, but which had upon me the effect
a bag full of napoleons might have upon a beggar if
swung under his nose by an insolent banker.

" Ah, señorita !" I said at last, beginning to lose
patience, " what matters it, after all, whether cities
are beautiful or not ? Those who are born in them
think nothing of it, and the traveller still less. I
arrived at Cordova yesterday : it is a beautiful city,
without doubt. Well—will you believe it ?—I have
already forgotten all that I have seen ; I no longer
wish to see anything ; I do not even know what city
I am in. Palaces, mosques, they make me laugh.
When you have a consuming fire in your heart, do
you go to the mosque to quench it ?—Excuse me,

will you move back a little ?—When you feel such a madness that you could grind up a plate with your teeth, do you go to look at palaces? Believe me, the traveller's life is a sad one. It is a penance of the hardest sort. It is torture. It is . . ." A prudent blow with her fan closed my mouth, which was going too far both in words and action. I attacked the chop.

"Poor fellow!" murmured the Andalusian with a laugh after she had given a glance around. "Are all the Italians as ardent as you?"

"How should I know? Are all the Andalusians as beautiful as you?"

The girl laid her hand on the table.

"Take that hand away," I said.

"Why?" she asked.

"Because I want to eat in peace."

"Eat with one hand."

"Ah!"

I seemed to be pressing the little hand of a girl of six; my knife fell to the ground; a dark veil settled upon the chop.

Suddenly my hand was empty: I opened my eyes, saw the girl all disturbed, and looked behind me. Gracious Heavens! There was a handsome young fellow, with a stylish little jacket, tight breeches, and a velvet cap. Oh terrors! a *torero!* I gave a start as if I had felt two *banderillas de yfuego* planted in my neck.

"I see it at a glance," said I to myself, like the man at the comedy; and one could not fail to understand. The girl, slightly embarrassed, made the introduction: "An Italian passing through Cordova," and she hastened to add, "who wants to know when the train leaves for Seville."

The *torero*, who had frowned at first sight of me, was reassured, told me the hour of departure, sat down, and entered into a friendly conversation. I asked for the news of the last bull-fight at Cordova: he was a *banderillero*, and he gave me a minute description of the day's sport. The girl in the mean time was gathering flowers from the vases in the *patio*. I finished my meal, offered a glass of Malaga to the *torero*, drank to the fortunate planting of all his *banderillas*, paid my bill (three *pesetas*, which included the beautiful eyes, you understand), and then, putting on a bold front, so as to dispel the least shadow of suspicion from the mind of my formidable rival, I said to the girl, "*Señorita!* one can refuse nothing to those who are taking leave. To you I am like a dying man; you will never see me again; you will never hear my name spoken: then let me take some memento; give me that bunch of flowers."

"Take it," said the girl; "I picked it for you."

She glanced at the *torero*, who gave a nod of approval.

"I thank you with all my heart," I replied as I

turned to leave. They both accompanied me to the door.

"Have you bull-fights in Italy?" asked the young man.

"Oh heavens! no, not yet!"

"Too bad! Try to make them popular in Italy also, and I will come to *banderillar* at Rome."

"I will do all in my power.—*Señorita*, have the goodness to tell me your name, so that I may bid you good-bye."

"Consuelo."

"God be with you, Consuelo!"

"God be with you, *Señor Italiano!*"

And I went out into the lonely little street.

There are no remarkable Arabian monuments to be seen in the neighborhood of Cordova, although at one time the whole valley was covered with magnificent buildings. Three miles to the south of the city, on the side of the mountain, rose the Medina Az-Zahra, the city of flowers, one of the most marvellous architectural works of the caliph Abdurrahman, begun by the caliph himself in honor of his favorite Az-Zahra. The foundations were laid in the year 936, and ten thousand workmen labored on the edifice for twenty-five years. The Arabian poets celebrated Medina Az-Zahra as the most splendid of royal palaces and the most delightfull garden in the world. It was not an edifice, but a vast chain of palaces, gardens, courts, colonnades, and towers. There were rare plants from Syria—the fantastic playing of lofty fountains, streams of water flowing in the shade of palm trees, and great basins overflowing with quicksilver, which reflected the rays of the sun like lakes of fire; doors of ebony and ivory studded with gems; thousands of columns of the most precious marbles; great airy balconies; and between the innumerable multitudes of statues twelve images of animals of massy gold, gleaming with pearls, sprinkling sweetened water from their mouths and noses. In this vast palace swarmed thousands of servants, slaves, and women, and hither from every part of the world came poets and musicians. And yet this same Abdurrahman III., who lived among all these delights, who reigned for fifty years, who was powerful, glorious, and fortunate in every circumstance and enterprise, wrote before his death that during his long reign he had been happy only fourteen days, and his fabulous city of flowers seventy-four years after the laying of its first stone was invaded, sacked, and burned by a barbarian horde, and to-day there remain only a few stones which hardly recall its name.

Of another splendid city, called Zahira, which rose to the east of Cordova, built by the powerful Almansur, governor of the kingdom, not even the ruins remain: a handful of rebels laid it in ashes a little while after the death of its founder.

"All returns to the great ancient mother."

Instead of taking a drive around Cordova, I simply wandered here and there, weaving fancies from the names of the streets, which to me is one of the greatest pleasures in which a traveller may indulge in a foreign city. Cordova, *alma ingeniorum parens*, could write at every street-corner the name of an artist or an illustrious author born within her walls; to give her due honor, she has remembered them all with maternal gratitude. You find the little square of Seneca and the house where he may have been born; the street of Ambrosio Morales, the historian of Charles V., who continued the *Chronicle General of Spain* commenced by Florian d'Ocampo; the street of Pablo de Cespedes, painter, architect, sculptor, antiquary, and the author of a didactic poem, "The Art of Painting," unfortunately not finished, though adorned with splendid passages. He was an ardent enthusiast of Michelangelo, whose works he had admired in Italy, and in his poem he addressed a hymn of praise to him which is one of the most beautiful passages in Spanish poetry, and, in spite of myself, the last verses have slipped from my pen, which every Italian, even if he does not know the sister language, can appreciate and understand. He believes, he tells the reader, that one cannot find the perfection of painting anywhere except

"Que en aquela escelente obra espantosa
Mayor de cuantas se han jamas pintado,

Que hizo el Buonarrota de su mano
Divina, en el etrusco Vaticano !

"Cual nuevo Prometeo en alto vuelo
  Alzándose, estendió los alas tanto,
  Que puesto encima el estrellado cielo
  Una parte alcanzò del fuego santo ;
  Con que tornando enriquecido al suelo
  Con nueva maravilla y nuevo espanto,
  Diò vida con eternos resplandores
  À marmoles, à bronces, à colores.
  ¡ O mas que mortal hombre !   ¿ Angel divino
  O cual te nomaré ?   No humano cierto
  Es tu ser, que del cerco empireo vino
  Al estilo y pincel vida y concierto :
  Tu monstraste à los hombres el camino
  Por mil edades escondido, incierto
  De la reina virtud ; a ti se debe
  Honra que en cierto dia el sol renueve."

"In that excellent marvellous work, greater than all that has ever been painted, which Buonarroti made with his divine hand in the Etruscan Vatican!

"Look how the new Prometheus, rising in lofty flight, extends his wings so wide that above the starry sky he has obtained a part of the celestial fire; with it, returning, he enriched the earth with new marvels and new surprises, giving life, with eternal splendors, to marble, bronze, and colors. More than mortal man! angel divine! or what shall I call thee?   Surely thou art not human, who from the empyrean circle came, bringing life and harmony to chisel and brush!   Thou hast shown men the road hidden for a thousand ages, uncertain of the sovereign virtue; to thee belongs honor which one day the sun will bestow."

Murmuring these lines, I came out into the street of Juan de Mena, the Ennius of Spain, as his compatriots call him, the author of a phantasmagorial poem called "The Labyrinth," an imitation of *The Divina Commedia* very famous in its day, and in truth not without some pages of inspired and noble poetry, but, on the whole, cold and overloaded with pedantic mysticism. John II., king of Castile, went mad over this " Labyrinth," kept it beside the missal in his cabinet, and carried it with him to the hunt; but witness the caprice of a king! The poem had only three hundred stanzas, and to John II. this number seemed too small, and do you know the reason? It was this: the year contains three hundred and sixty-five days, and it seemed to him that there ought to be as many stanzas in the poem as there are days in the year, and so he besought the poet to compose sixty-five other stanzas, and the poet complied with his request—most cheerfully, the flatterer!—to gain an occasion for flattering still more, although he had already flattered his sovereign to the extent of asking him to correct the poem.

From the street of Juan de Mena I passed into the street of Gongora, the Marini of Spain, and no less a genius than he, but perhaps one who corrupted the literature of his country even more than Marini corrupted that of Italy, for he spoiled, abused, and corrupted the language in a thousand ways : for this reason Lope de Vega wittily makes a poet of the Gongorist school ask one of his hearers, "Do you understand me?"—"Yes," he replies; and the poet retorts, "You lie! for I do not even understand myself." But Lope himself is not entirely free from Gongorism, for he has the courage to write that Tasso was only the rising of Marini's sun; nor is Calderon entirely free of it, nor some other great men. But enough of poetry : I must not digress.

After the siesta I hunted up my two companions, who took me through the suburbs of the city, and here, for the first time, I saw men and women of the true Andalusian type as I had imagined them, with eyes, coloring, and attitudes like the Arabians, and here too, for the first time, I heard the real speech of the Andalusian people, softer and more musical than in the Castiles, and also gayer and more imaginative, and accompanied by livelier gestures. I asked my companions whether that report about Andalusia is true, affirming that with their early physical development vice is more common, manners more voluptuous, and passion less restrained. "Too true," they replied, giving explanations, descriptions, and citing cases which I forbear to repeat. On returning to the city they took me to a splendid casino, with gardens and magnificent rooms, in one of which, the largest and richest, adorned with paintings of all the illustrious men of Cordova, rises a sort of stage where the poets stand to read their works on evenings appointed for public contests of genius; and the victors receive a laurel crown from the hands of the most beautiful and cultured girls in the city, who, crowned with roses, look on from a semi-circle of seats. That evening I had the pleasure of meeting several young Cordovese ardently attached, as they say in Spain, to the cultivation of the Muses —frank, courteous, and vivacious, with a medley of verses in their heads, and a smattering of Italian literature; and so imagine how from dusk to midnight, through those mysterious streets, which from the first evening had made my head whirl, there was a constant, noisy interchange of sonnets, hymns, and ballads in the two languages, from Petrarch to Prati, from Cervantes to Zorilla; and a delightful conversation closed and sealed by many cordial hand-clasps and eager promises to write, to send books, to come to Italy, to visit Spain again, etc. etc.—merely words, as is always the case, but words not less dear on that account.

In the morning I left for Seville. At the station I saw Frascuelo, Lagartijo, Cuco, and the whole band of *toreros* from Madrid, who saluted me with a benevolent look of protection. I hurried into a dusty carriage, and as the train moved off and my eyes rested on Cordova for the last time, I bade the city adieu in the lines of the Arabian poet—a little too tropical, if you will, for the taste of a European, but, after all, admirable for the occasion :

"Adieu, Cordova! Would that my life were as long as Noah's, that I might live for ever within thy walls! Would that I had the treasures of Pharaoh, to spend them upon wine and the beautiful women of Cordova with the gentle eyes which invite kisses!"

SEVILLE.

SEVILLE.

THE journey from Cordova to Seville does not awaken a sense of astonishment, as does that from Toledo to Cordova, but it is even more beautiful: there are continuous orange-orchards, boundless olive-groves, hills clothed with vineyards, and meadows carpeted with flowers. A few miles from Cordova one sees the ruined towers of the frowning castle of Almodovar standing on a very high rock-platform, which overlooks a vast extent of the surrounding country; at Hornachuelos another old castle on the summit of a hill, in the midst of a lonely, melancholy landscape; and then, beyond, the white city of Palma, hidden in a dense orange-grove, which is surrounded in its turn by a circle of truck-farms and flower-gardens. As the train runs on one is carried through the midst of golden fields of grain, bordered by long hedges of Indian fig trees and rows of dwarf palms, and dotted with groves of pine and frequent orchards of fruit-bearing trees; and at short intervals there are hills and castles, roaring streams, the slender village belfries hidden among the trees, and the purple peaks of distant mountains.

Most beautiful of all are the little country-houses scattered along the road. I do not remember to have seen a single one of them that was not as white as snow. The house was white, the neighboring well-curb was white, the little wall around the kitchen-garden was white, as were also the two posts of the garden-gate; everything seemed as if it had been whitewashed the day before. Some of these houses have one or two mullioned windows of Moorish design; others have arabesques over the door; and still others roofs covered with variegated tiles like Arabian houses. Here and there through the fields one sees the red-and-white capes of the peasants, velvet hats against the green grass, and sashes of all colors. The peasants whom one sees in the furrows and those who run to see the train pass are dressed in the costumes of forty years ago as they are represented in paintings: they wear velvet hats with very broad brims which roll slightly back, with little crowns like a sugar-loaf; short jackets, open waistcoats, breeches gathered in at the knee like those of the priests, gaiters which almost meet the breeches, and sashes around the waist. This style of dress, picturesque but inconvenient, is exceedingly becoming to the slender figures of these men, who prefer discomfort, if it be attended by beauty, to comfort without it, and who

spend half an hour every morning adorning themselves, besides the time required to get into a pair
of tight breeches which will display a shapely thigh
and a well-turned leg. They have nothing in common with our Northern peasant of the hard face and
dull eye. Their great black eyes meet your own
with a smile, as if they would say, "Don't you
remember me?" They cast daring glances at the
ladies who put their heads out of the windows, run
to fetch a match before you have so much as asked
for it, sometimes answer your questions in rhyme,
and are even capable of laughing to show their
white teeth.

At Rinconado the campanile of the cathedral of
Seville comes into view in a line with the railroad,
and to the right, beyond the Guadalquivir, one sees
the beautiful low hills, covered with olive-groves, at
the foot of which lie the ruins of Italica. The train
rolled on, and I said to myself, under my breath,
speaking faster and faster as the houses became
thicker, with that suspense, full of longing and
delight, which one feels on approaching the doorway of one's love, "Seville! this is Seville! The
queen of Andalusia is at hand, the Athens of Spain,
the mother of Murillo, the city of poets and lovers,
the storied Seville, whose name I have pronounced
from a child with a sentiment of loving sympathy!
What should I have given a few years since to have
seen it? No, it is not a dream! Those are really

the houses of Seville; those peasants yonder are Sevillians; that campanile which I see is the Giralda! I am at Seville! How strange! It makes me laugh! What is my mother doing at this moment? Would that she were here! Would that this friend and that were here! It is a sin to be alone! See the white houses, the gardens, the streets. . . . We are in the city. . . . It is time to get out. . . . Ah! how beautiful is life!"

I went to a hotel, threw down my valise in the *patio*, and began to stroll about the city. It seemed like seeing Cordova over again, on a large scale, embellished and enriched; the streets are wider, the houses higher, the *patios* more spacious, but the general appearance of the city is the same: there is the same spotless white, the same intricate network of streets, everywhere the fragrance of orange-blossoms, that subtile air of mystery, that Oriental atmosphere, filling one's heart with a delicious sense of amorous melancholy, and calling to mind a thousand fancies, desires, and visions of a distant world, a new life, an unknown people, and an earthly paradise of love, pleasure, and content. In those streets one reads the history of the city: every balcony, every fragment of sculpture, every lonely crossway, recalls some nocturnal adventure of a king, the inspiration of a poet, the romance of a beauty, an amour, a duel, an abduction, a story, or a festival. Here a memento of Maria de Padilla, there one of

Don Pedro; yonder of Cervantes, Columbus, Saint Theresa, Velasquez, or Murillo. A column tells of the Roman dominion; a tower, the splendor of Charles V.'s monarchy; and an alcazar, the magnificence of the Arabian court. Beside the modest white cottages rise sumptuous marble palaces; the little tortuous streets open into vast squares full of orange trees; from silent, deserted corners one enters with a short turn a street filled with a noisy crowd: and wherever one passes one sees on the opposite side the graceful lattices of the *patios*, flowers, statues, fountains, flights of stairs, walls covered with arabesques, small Moorish windows, and slender columns of costly marble; and at every window and in every garden little women clothed in white, half hidden, like timid nymphs, among the leaves of grapevines and rosebushes.

Passing from street to street, I came at length to the bank of the Guadalquivir, close to the avenues of the Christina promenade, which is to Seville what the Lung d'arno is to Florence. Here one enjoys a charming spectacle.

I first approached the famous Torre del Oro. This famous tower was called the Golden, either because it received the gold which the Spanish ships brought from America or because King Don Pedro hid his treasures there. It is an octagonal structure of three stories, growing smaller as they ascend, crowned with battlements and washed by the river.

The story runs that this tower was built in Roman times, and that for a long period the king's most beautiful favorite dwelt there after it had been joined to the Alcazar by an edifice which was torn away to make room for the Christina promenade.

This promenade extends from the ducal palace of Montpensier to the Torre del Oro. It is entirely shaded with Oriental plane trees, oaks, cypresses, willows, poplars. and other trees of northern latitudes, which the Andalusians admire, as we admire the palms and aloes of the plains of Piedmont and Lombardy. A great bridge spans the river and leads to the suburb of Triana, from which one sees the first houses on the opposite bank. A long line of ships, coasting vessels, and barges extends along the river, and from the Torre del Oro to the ducal palace there is a coming and going of rowboats. The sun was setting. A crowd of ladies filled the avenues, groups of workmen were crossing the bridge, the workmen on the ships labored more busily, a band of music was playing among the trees, the river was rose-colored, the air was fragrant with the perfume of flowers, the sky seemed all on fire.

I returned to the city and enjoyed the marvellous spectacle of Seville by night. All the *patios* were illuminated—those of the humble houses with a half light, which gave them an air of mysterious beauty, those of the palaces, full of little flames which were

reflected in the mirrors and flashed like jets of quicksilver in the spray of the fountains, and shone with
a thousand colors on the marbles of the vestibules,
the mosaics of the walls, the glass of the doors, and
the crystal of the candlesticks. Inside one saw a
crowd of ladies, everywhere one heard the sound of
laughter, low voices, and music; one seemed to be
passing through so many ball-rooms; from every
door flowed a stream of light, fragrance, and harmony; the streets were crowded; among the trees
of the squares, in the avenues, at the end of the
narrow streets, and on the balconies,—everywhere
were seen white skirts fluttering, vanishing, and re-
appearing in the darkness, and little heads ornamented with flowers peeped coquettishly from the
windows; groups of young men broke through the
crowd with merry shouts; people called to each
other and talked from window to street, and everywhere were rapid motion, shouting, laughter, and
festal gaiety. Seville was simply an immense garden in which revelled a people intoxicated with
youth and love.

Such moments are very sad ones for a stranger.
I remember that I could have struck my head
against the wall. I wandered here and there almost
abashed, with hanging head and sad heart, as if all
that crowd was amusing itself for the sole purpose
of insulting my loneliness and melancholy. It was
too late to present my letters of introduction, too

early to go to bed: I was the slave of that crowd
and that gaiety, and was obliged to endure it for
many hours. I found a solace in resolving not to
look at the faces of the women, but I could not
always keep my resolve, and when my eyes inad-
vertently met two black pupils the wound, because
so unexpected, was more grievous than if I had en-
countered the danger more boldly. Yes, I was
in the midst of those wonderfully famous women
of Seville! I saw them pass on the arms of their
husbands and lovers; I touched their dresses,
breathed their perfume, heard the sound of their
soft speech, and the blood leaped to my head like a
flame of fire. Fortunately, I remembered to have
heard from a Sevillian at Madrid that the Italian
consul was in the habit of spending the evening at
the shop of his son, a merchant; I sought out the
shop, entered, and found the consul, and as I handed
him a letter from a friend I said, with a dramatic air
which made him laugh, " Dear sir, protect me; Seville has terrified me."

At midnight the appearance of the city was un-
changed: the crowd and light had not disappeared;
I returned to the hotel and locked my door with the
intention of going to bed. Worse and worse! The
windows of my room opened on a square where
crowds of people were swarming around an orches-
tra that played without interruption, when the music
finally ended the guitars commenced, together with the

cries of the water-carriers and snatches of song and laughter; the whole night through there was noise enough to wake the dead. I had a dream at once delightful and tantalizing, but rather more tantalizing than delightful. I seemed to be tied to the bed by a very long tress of dark hair twisted into a thousand knots, and felt on my lips a mouth of burning coals which sucked my breath, and around my neck two vigorous little hands which were crushing my head against the handle of a guitar.

The following morning I went at once to see the cathedral.

To adequately describe this measureless edifice one should have at hand a collection of the most superlative adjectives and all the most extravagant similes which have come from the pens of the grand writers of every country whenever they have described something of prodigious height, enormous size, appalling depth, and incredible grandeur. When I talk to my friends about it, I too, like the Mirabeau of Victor Hugo, involuntarily make *un colossal mouvement d'epaules*, puff out my throat, and gradually raise my voice, like Tommaso Salvini in the tragedy of *Samson* when, in tones which make the parquet tremble, he says that he feels his strength returning to his limbs. To talk of the cathedral of Seville tires one like playing a great wind instrument or carrying on a conversation across a roaring torrent.

The cathedral of Seville stands alone in the centre of a vast square, and consequently one can measure its vastness at a single glance. At the first moment I thought of the famous motto which the chapter of the primitive church adopted on the eighth of July, 1401, when they decreed the erection of the new cathedral: "Let us build a monument which will make posterity declare that we were mad." Those reverend canons did not fail in their intention. But one must enter to be sure of this.

The exterior of the cathedral is grand and magnificent, but not to be compared with the interior. The façade is lacking: a high wall surrounds the entire building like a fortress. However much one walks around and looks at it, one cannot succeed in fixing in one's mind a single outline which, like the preface of a book, will give a clear conception of the design of the work; one admires and occasionally breaks out in the exclamation, "It is stupendous!" but it does not please, and one hurries into the church, hoping to feel a sentiment of deeper admiration.

On first entering one is amazed, and feels as if one were lost in an abyss, and for some moments the eye can only describe immense curves through that vast space, as if to assure you that the sight is real and that fancy is not deceiving you. Then you approach one of the pilasters, measure it, and look at the others in the distance: they are as massive as

towers, and yet they look so slender that one trem-
bles to think the edifice is resting on them. You
run from one to another with a rapid glance, follow
their lines from pavement to vaulted arch, and seem
to be able to count the moments which it would take
for the eye to climb them. There are five naves,
each of which would form a great church, and in the
central nave one could build another high cathedral
with its cupola and belfry. Altogether they form
sixty light, noble vaults which seem to be slowly
expanding and rising as one looks at them. Everything in this cathedral is enormous. The great
chapel in the middle of the principal nave, so high
that it almost touches the roof, seems like a chapel
built for giant priests, to whose knees the common
altars would scarcely reach; the Easter candle
seems like the mast of a ship, the bronze candle-
stick which supports it, like the pilaster of a church;
the organs are like houses; the choir is a museum
of sculpture and carving which alone deserves a
day's study. The chapels are worthy of the church:
in them are scattered the masterpieces of sixty-
seven sculptors and thirty-eight painters. Montcgna,
Zurbaran, Murillo, Valdes, Herrera, Boldan, Roelas,
and Campana have left a thousand immortal traces
of their handiwork. The chapel of Saint Ferdinand, which contains the tombs of this king, his
wife Beatrice, Alfonso the Wise, the celebrated
minister Florida Blanca, and other illustrious per-

sonages, is one of the richest and most beautiful.
The body of King Ferdinand, who rescued Seville
from the dominion of the Arabs, clothed in his coat-
of-mail with crown and royal robe, rests in a crystal
casket covered with a pall; on one side lies the
sword which he wore on the day of his entrance into
Seville; on the other, the staff, an emblem of authority. In this same chapel is preserved a little
ivory Virgin which the sainted king carried with
him to war, and other relics of great value. In the
other chapels there are great marble altars, Gothic
tombs, statues of stone, wood, and silver enclosed
in large glass cases, with the breast and hands
covered with diamonds and rubies; there are also
magnificent paintings, but, unfortunately, the dim
light which falls from the high windows does not
make them clear enough to be enjoyed in all their
beauty.

From the examination of the chapels, paintings,
and sculptures one returns unwearied to admire the
cathedral in its grand and, if one may say, its formidable aspect. After climbing to those dizzy
heights one's glance and thoughts, as if exhausted
by the effort, fall back to the earth to gather new
strength for another ascent. And the images which
multiply in one's head correspond to the vastness of
the basilica—measureless angels, heads of enormous
cherubim, great wings like the sails of a ship, and
the fluttering of immense white robes. The impres-

sion produced by this cathedral is wholly religious, but it is not depressing: it is that sentiment which bears the thought into interminable spaces and the awful silences where the thoughts of Leopardi lost themselves; it is a sentiment full of yearning and holy boldness, that delightful shudder which one feels on the brink of a precipice, the turbulence and confusion of great thoughts, the divine fear of the infinite.

As the cathedral is the most various of Spain (since the Gothic, Germanic, Græco-Roman, Moorish, and, as it is vulgarly called, the plateresque styles of architecture, have each left their individual impress upon it), it is also the richest and has the greatest privileges. In the times of greater clerical power they burned in it every year twenty thousand pounds of wax; in it every day were celebreted five hundred masses on eighty altars; the wine consumed in the sacrifice amounted to the incredible quantity of eighteen thousand seven hundred and fifty litres. The canons had trains of male attendants like monarchs, came to church in splendid carriages drawn by superb horses, and while they were celebrating mass had priests to fan them with enormous fans adorned with feathers and pearls—a direct concession from the Pope of which some avail themselves even in this day. One need not speak of the festivals of Holy Week, which are still

famous the world over, and to which people gather
from all parts of Europe.

But the most curious privilege of the cathedral
of Seville is the so-called dance *de los seises*, which
takes place every evening at dusk for eight consecutive days after the festival of *Corpus Domini*.
I was in Seville during those days, and went to see
it, and it seems to me worth describing.   From
what had been told me I expected to see a scandalous piece of buffoonery, and entered the church
with my mind prepared for a feeling of indignation
at the desecration of the sanctuary.   The church
was dark; only the great chapel was lighted; a
crowd of kneeling women filled the space between
the chapel and the choir.   Some priests were sitting
to the right and left of the altar; in front of the
altar-steps was spread a great carpet; two lines of
boys from eight to thirteen years of age, dressed
like Spanish cavaliers of the Middle Ages, with
plumed hats and white stockings, were drawn up,
one before the other, facing the altar.   At a signal
from a priest a soft strain from violins broke the
profound silence of the church, and the two rows of
boys advanced with the step of a contra-dance, and
began to divide, intermingle, separate, and come together again with a thousand graceful movements, and
then all together they broke into a harmonious musical chant, which echoed through the gloom of the
vast cathedral like the singing of an angelic choir;

and a moment later they began to accompany the dance and the chant with tamborines. No religious ceremony has ever moved me like this. It is impossible to express the effect produced by those young voices under those immense domes, those little creatures at the foot of the towering altars, that dance, solemn and almost humble, the ancient costume, the kneeling crowd, and the surrounding gloom. I left the church with my soul calmed as if I had been praying.

A very curious anecdote is related in connection with this ceremony. Two centuries ago an archbishop of Seville, who regarded the dance and tamborines as unworthy instruments of praising God, wished to prohibit the ceremony. Everything was thrown into confusion: the people protested; the canons made themselves heard; the archbishop was obliged to appeal to the Pope. The Pope, whose curiosity was aroused, wished to see this silly dance with his own eyes, that he might decide intelligently in the matter. The boys in their cavalier dress were taken to Rome, received at the Vatican, and made to dance and sing before His Holiness. His Holiness laughed, did not disapprove, and, wishing to give one knock on the hoop and another on the barrel, and so to satisfy the canons without offending the archbishop, decreed that the boys should continue to dance so long as the clothes which they then wore lasted; after that time the ceremony was to be abolished. The archbishop laughed in his beard, if he had one; the canons laughed too, as if they had already found the way to outwit both the Pope and the archbishop. And, in fact, they renew some part of the boys' dress every year, so that the whole garment can never be said to have worn out, and the archbishop, as a scrupulous man, who observed the commands of the Pope to the letter, could not oppose the repetition of the ceremony. So they continued to dance, and they dance and will dance so long as it pleases the canons and the Lord.

As I was leaving the church a sacristan made me a sign, led me behind the choir, and pointed out a tablet in the pavement, upon which I read an inscription which stirred my heart. Under that stone lay the bones of Ferdinand Columbus, the son of Christopher, who was born at Cordova, and died at Seville on the twelfth of July, 1536, in the fiftieth year of his age. Under the inscription run some Latin verses with the following significance:

" Of what avail is it that I have bathed the entire universe with my sweat, that I have three times passed through the New World discovered by my father, that I have adorned the banks of the gentle Beti, and preferred my simple taste to riches, that I might again draw around thee the divinities of the Castalian spring, and offer thee the treasures already gathered by Ptolemy,—if thou, passing this stone in silence, returnest no salute to my father and givest no thought to me ?"

The sacristan, who knew more about the inscription than I did, explained it to me. Ferdinand Columbus was in his early youth a page of Isabella the Catholic and of the prince Don Juan; he travelled to the Indies with his father and his brother the admiral Don Diego, followed the emperor Charles V. in his wars, made other voyages to Asia, Africa, and America, and everywhere collected with infinite care and at great expense the most precious books, from which he composed a library which passed after his death into the hands of the chapter of the cathedral, and remains intact under the famous name of the Columbian Library. Before his death he wrote these same Latin verses which are inscribed on the tablet of his tomb, and expressed a desire to be buried in the cathedral. In the last moments of his life he had a vessel full of ashes brought to him and sprinkled his face with them, pronouncing as he did so the words of Holy Writ, *Memento homo quia pulvis es*, chanted the *Te Deum*, smiled, and expired with the serenity of a saint. I was at once seized with a desire to visit the library and left the church.

A guide stopped me on the threshold to ask me if I had seen the *Patio de los Naranjos*—the Court of Oranges—and, as I had not done so, he conducted me thither. The Court of Oranges lies to the north of the cathedral, surrounded by a great embattled wall. In the centre rises a fountain encircled by an orange-grove, and on one side along the wall is a

marble pulpit, from which, according to the tradition, Vincenzo Ferrer is said to have preached. In
the area of this court, which is very large, rose the
ancient mosque, which is thought to have been built
toward the end of the twelfth century. There is
not the least trace of it now. In the shade of the
orange trees around the margins of the basin the
good Sevillians come to take the air in the burning
noons of summer, and only the delightful verdure
and the perfumed air remain as memorials of the
voluptuous paradise of Mohammed, while now and
then a beautiful girl with great dark eyes darts between the distant trees.

The famous Giralda of the cathedral of Seville is
an ancient Moorish tower, built, it is affirmed, in the
year one thousand after the design of the architect
Geber, the inventor of algebra. The upper part has
been changed since Spain was reconquered, and has
been rebuilt like a Christian bell-tower, but it will
always retain its Moorish appearance, and, after all,
is prouder of the banished standards of the van-
quished than of the cross recently planted upon it by
the victors. It is a monument which produces a
strange sensation: it makes one smile; it is measureless and imposing as an Egyptian pyramid, and
at the same time light and graceful as a summer-
house. It is a square brick tower of a mellow rose-
color, unadorned to a certain height, and from that
point up ornamented with mullioned Moorish win-

dows, which appear here and there like the windows of a house provided with balconies, and give it a very beautiful appearance. From the platform, which was formerly covered by a variegated roof surmounted by an iron pole which supported four enormous golden balls, now rises the Christian bell-tower in three stories, the first of which is taken up by the bells, the second is encircled by a balcony, and the third consists of a sort of cupola upon which, like a weather-vane, turns a colossal gilded statue which represents Faith, with a palm in one hand and a banner in the other. This statue is visible a long distance from Seville, and flashes when the sun strikes it like an enormous ruby in the crown of a gigantic king, who sweeps with his glance the entire valley of Andalusia.

I climbed all the way to the top, and was there amply rewarded for the fatigue of the ascent. Seville, all white like a city of marble, encircled by a diadem of gardens, groves, and avenues, surrounded by a landscape dotted with villas, lay open to the view in all the wealth of its Oriental beauty. The Guadalquivir, freighted with ships, divides and embraces it in a majestic curve. Here the Torre del Oro casts its graceful shadow on the azure waters of the river; there the Alcazar rears its frowning towers; yonder the gardens of Montpensier raise above the roofs of the building an enormous mass of verdure: one's glance penetrates the bull-ring, the

public gardens, the *patios* of the homes, the cloisters
of the churches, and all the streets which converge
toward the cathedral; in the distance appear the
villages of Santi Ponce, Algaba, and others which
whiten the slopes of the hills; to the right of the
Guadalquivir the great suburb of Triana; on one
side along the horizon the broken peaks of the Sierra
Morena; and in the opposite direction other mountains enlivened by infinite azure tints; and over all
this marvellous panorama the clearest, most trans-
parent, and entrancing sky which has ever smiled
upon the face of man.

I descended from the Giralda and went to see the
Columbian Library, located in an old building beside
the Court of Oranges.   After I had seen a collection
of missals, Bibles, and ancient manuscripts, one of
which is attributed to Alfonso the Wise, entitled
" The Book of the Treasure," written with the most
scrupulous care in the ancient Spanish language, I
saw—let me repeat it, I saw—I, with my own
moist eyes, as I pressed my hand on my beating
heart—I saw a book, a treatise on cosmography and
astronomy in Latin, with the margins covered with
notes written in the hand of Christopher Columbus!
He had studied that book while he revolved his
great design in his mind, had pored over its pages
in the night-watches, had touched it perhaps with
his divine forehead in those exhausting vigils when
sometimes he bent over the parchments with utter

weariness and bathed them with his sweat. It is a tremendous thought! But there is something better. I saw a writing in the hand of Columbus in which are collected all the prophecies of the ancient writers, sacred and profane, in regard to the discovery of the New World, written, it is said, to induce the sovereigns of Spain to provide the means to carry out his enterprise. There is, among others, a passage from the *Medea* of Seneca, which runs: *Venient annis saecula seris, quibus oceanus vincula rerum laxet et ingens pateat tellus.* And in the volume of Seneca, which may also be found in the Columbian Library, alongside of this passage there is a note by Ferdinand Columbus, which says: " This prophecy was fulfilled by my father, the admiral Christopher Columbus, in the year 1492." My eyes filled with tears; I wished I were alone, that I might have kissed those books, have tired myself out turning and re-turning their leaves between my hands, have detached a tiny fragment, and carried it with me as a sacred thing. Christopher Columbus! I have seen his characters! I have touched the leaves which he has touched! I have felt him very near me! On leaving the library, I know not why—I could have leaped into the midst of the flames to rescue a child, I could have stripped myself to clothe a beggar, I could joyfully have made any sacrifice—I was so rich!

After the library the Alcazar, but before reaching

it, although it is in the same square as the cathedral, I felt for the first time what the Andalusian sun is like. Seville is the hottest city of Spain, it was the hottest hour of the day, and I found myself in the hottest part of the city ; there was a flood of light ; not a door, not a window, was open, not a soul astir ; if I had been told that Seville was uninhabited, I should have believed it. I crossed the square slowly with half-shut eyes and wrinkled face, with the sweat coursing in great drops down my cheeks and breast, while my hands seemed to have been dipped in a bucket of water. On nearing the Alcazar I saw a sort of booth belonging to a water-carrier, and dashed under it headlong, like a man fleeing from a shower of stones. I took a little breathing-spell, and went on toward the Alcazar.

The Alcazar, the ancient palace of the Moorish kings, is one of the best-preserved monuments in Spain. From the outside it looks like a fortress : it is entirely surrounded by high walls, embattled towers, and old houses, which form two spacious courtyards in front of the façade. The façade is bare and severe, like the rest of the exterior ; the gate is adorned with gilded and painted arabesques, between which one sees a Gothic inscription which refers to the time when the Alcazar was restored by order of King Don Pedro. The Alcazar, in fact, although a Moorish palace, is the work of Christian rather than of Moorish kings. It is not known

exactly in what year it was built: it was reconstructed by King Abdelasio toward the end of the
twelfth century, conquered by King Ferdinand toward the middle of the thirteenth century; altered
a second time, in the following century, by King Don
Pedro; and then occupied for longer or shorter
periods by nearly all the kings of Castile; and
finally selected by Charles V. as the place for the
celebration of his marriage with the infanta of
Portugal. The Alcazar has witnessed the loves
and crimes of three generations of kings; every
stone awakens a memory and guards a secret.

You enter, cross two or three rooms in which
there remains little of the Moorish excepting the
vaulted ceiling and the mosaics around the walls,
and come out into a court where you stand speechless with wonder. A portico of very delicate arches
extends along the four sides, supported by slender
marble columns, joined two by two, and arches and
walls and windows and doors are covered with carv-
ings, mosaics, and arabesques most intricate and exquisite, here perforated like lace, there closely
woven and elaborate like embroidered tapestry,
yonder clinging and projecting like masses and
garlands of flowers; and, except the mosaics, which
are of a thousand colors, everything is white, clean,
and smooth as ivory. On the four sides are four
great doors, through which you enter the royal
apartments. Here wonder becomes enchantment:

whatever is richest, most various, and most splendid, whatever the most ardent fancy sees in its most ardent dreams, is to be found in these rooms. From pavement to the vaulted ceiling, around the doors, along the window-frames, in the most hidden corners, wherever one's glance falls, one sees such a luxuriance of ornaments in gold and precious stones, such a close network of arabesques and inscriptions, such a marvellous profusion of designs and colors, that one has scarcely taken twenty steps before one is amazed and confused, and the wearied eye wanders here and there searching for a hand's breadth of bare wall where it may flee and rest. In one of these rooms the guide pointed out a red spot which covered a good part of the marble pavement, and said in a solemn voice, " These are the blood-stains of Don Fadrique, grand master of the order of Santiago, who was killed on this very spot, in the year 1358, by order of his brother, King Don Pedro."

I remember that when I heard these words I looked in the face of the custodian, as if to say, " Come, let us be going," and that good man answered in a dry tone,

" *Caballero*, if I had told you to believe this thing on my word, you would have had every reason to doubt; but when you can see the thing with your very eyes, I may be wrong, but—it seems to me . . ."

" Yes," I hastened to say—"yes, it is blood : I believe it, I see it; let's say no more about it."

But if one can be playful over the blood-spots, one cannot be so over the story of the crime; the sight of the place revives in the mind all the most horrible details. Through the great gilded halls one seems to hear the echo of Don Fadrique's footsteps, followed by those of the bowmen armed with bludgeons; the palace is immersed in gloom; one hears no other sound save that of the executioners and their victim; Don Fadrique tries to enter the courtyard; Lopez de Padilla catches him; Fadrique throws him off and is in the court; he grasps his sword; curses on it ! the cross of the hilt is held fast in the mantle of the order of Santiago; the bowmen gain upon him; he has not time to unsheath the sword; he flees here and there, groping his way; Fernandez de Roa overtakes him and fells him with a blow of his club; the others run up and set upon him, and Fadrique dies in a pool of blood. . . .

But this sad recollection is lost among the thousand images of the sensuous Moorish kings. Those graceful little windows, where it seems as if you ought to see every other moment the languid face of an odalisque; those secret doors, at which you pause in spite of yourself, as if you heard the rustle of garments; those sleeping chambers of the sultans, shrouded in mysterious gloom, where you seem to hear only the confused amorous lament of all the maidens who there lost the flower of their virgin purity; that prodigal variety of color and line, which like a tumultuous and ever-changing harmony arouses the senses to such fantastic flights that you doubt whether you are waking or sleeping; that delicate and lovely architecture, all of slender columns, that seem like the arms of women; capricious arches, little rooms, arched ceilings crowded with ornaments hanging in the form of stalactites, icicles, and clusters of grapes, of as many colors as a flower-garden; —all this stirs your desire to sit down in the middle of one of those rooms and to press to your heart a lovely brown Andalusian head which will make you forget the world and time, and, with one long kiss that drinks away your life, give you eternal sleep.

On the ground floor the most beautiful room is the Hall of the Ambassadors, formed by four great arches which support a gallery with forty-four smaller arches, and above a beautiful cupola carved, painted, gilded, and chased with inimitable grace and fabulous splendor.

On the upper floor, where were the winter apartments, there remain only an oratory of Ferdinand and Isabella the Catholic, and a little room in which the king Don Pedro is said to have slept. From it one descends by a narrow mysterious staircase to the rooms where dwelt the famous Maria de Padilla, the favorite of Don Pedro, whom popular tradition accuses of instigating the king to kill his brother.

The gardens of the Alcazar are neither very large nor particularly beautiful, but the memories which they recall are of greater value than extent or beauty. In the shade of those orange trees and cypresses, to the murmur of those fountains, when the great white moon was shining in that limpid Andalusian sky, and the many groups of courtiers and slaves rested there, how many long sighs of ardent sultanas! how many lowly words from proud kings! what passionate loves and embraces! "Itimad, my love!" I murmured, thinking of the famous mistress of King Al-Motamid as I wandered from path to path as if following her phantom,—"Itimad," I repeated, "do not leave me alone in this silent paradise! Dost thou remember how thou camest to me? Thy wealth of hair fell over my shoulder, and dearer than the sword to the warrior wert thou to me! How beautiful thou art! Thy neck is soft and white as the swan's, and like berries are thy red, red lips! How marvellous is the perfection of thy beauty! How dear thou art, Itimad, my love! Thy kisses are like wine, and thy eyes, like wine, steal away my reason!"

While I was thus making my declarations of love with phrases and images stolen from the Arabian poets, at the very moment when I turned into a bypath all bordered with flowers, suddenly I felt a stream of water first on one leg and then on the other. I jumped aside, and received a spray in my face; I turned to the right, and felt another stream against my neck; to the left, another jet between my shoulders. I began to run: there was water under me and around me in every direction, in jets, streams, and spray; in a moment I was as wet as if I had been dipped in the bath-tub. Just as I opened my mouth to call for help it all subsided, and I heard a ringing laugh at the end of the garden. I turned and saw a young fellow leaning against a low wall looking at me as if he were saying, "How did you like it?" When I came out he showed me the spring he had touched to play this little joke, and comforted me with the assurance that the sun of Seville would not leave me long in that dripping condition, into which I had passed so rudely, alas! from the lovely arms of my sultana.

That evening, in spite of the voluptuous images which the Alcazar had called to my mind, I was sufficiently calm to contemplate the beauty of the women of Seville without fleeing to the arms of the consul for safety. I do not believe that the women of any other country are so bewitching as the fair Andalusians, not only because they tempt one into all sorts of mischief, but because they seem to have been made to be seized and carried away, so small, graceful, plump, elastic, and soft are they. Their little feet could both be put easily into one's coat-pocket, and with an arm one could lift them by the waist like babies, and by the mere pressure of the finger could bend them like willow wands. To their natural beauty they add the art of walking and looking in a way to turn one's head. They fly along, glide, and walk with a wave-like motion, and in a single moment, as they pass, they show a little foot, make you admire an arm or a slender waist, reveal two rows of the whitest teeth, and dart at you a long veiled glance that melts and dies in your own ; and on they go with an air of triumph, certain of having turned your blood topsy-turvy.

To form an idea of the beauty of the women of the people and the picturesqueness of their dress you must go by day to visit the tobacco-manufactory, which is one of the largest establishments of the kind in Europe and employs not less than five thousand hands. The building faces the vast gardens of the duke of Montpensier : almost all of the women work in three immense rooms, each divided into three parts by as many rows of pillars. The first view is astounding : there, all at once, eight hundred girls present themselves before one's eyes in groups of five or six, sitting around work-tables as close as possible, the farthest indistinct and the last scarcely visible ; all of them young and a few children—eight hundred jet-black heads and eight hundred brown faces from every province of Andalusia, from Jaen to Cadiz, from Granada to Seville !

One hears a buzzing as of a square full of people.

The walls, from one door to the other, in all three of the rooms are lined with skirts, shawls, kerchiefs, and scarfs; and—a very curious thing—that entire mass of garments, which would fill to overflowing a hundred old-clothes shops, presents two predominant colors, in two continuous lines one above the other, like the stripes of a very long flag—the black of the shawls above, and the red mixed with white, purple, and yellow—so that one seems to see an immense costumer's shop or an immense ball-room where the ballet-dancers, in order to be free, have hung on the walls every part of their dress which it is not absolutely necessary to wear. The girls put on these dresses when they go out, and wear old clothes to work in; but white and red predominate in those dresses also. The heat is insupportable, consequently they lighten their clothing as much as possible, and among those five thousand one will scarcely find fifty whose arms and shoulders the visitor may not contemplate at his pleasure, without counting the extraordinary cases which present themselves suddenly as one passes from room to room, behind the doors and columns, and around the distant corners. There are some very beautiful faces, and even those who are not beautiful have something about them which attracts one's glance and lingers in the memory—the complexion, the eyes, the brow, or the smile. Many of them, especially so-called *Gitane*, are as dark as dark mulattos and have protruding lips; others have eyes so large that a faithful picture of them would be considered a monstrous exaggeration; the greater part are small and well-formed, and all have a rose or carnation or some sort of wild flower in their hair. They are paid in proportion to the work they do, and the most skilful and industrious earn as much as three francs per day; the lazy ones—*las holgazanas*—sleep with their arms crossed on the table and their heads resting on their arms; mothers are working, and swinging a leg to which is bound a cord that rocks the cradle. From the cigar-room one passes to the cigarette-room, and from it to the box-factory, and from the box-factory to the packing-room, and in them all one sees the red skirts, black hair, and fine eyes. In each of those rooms how many stories of love, jealousy, despair, and misery! On leaving the factory one seems for some time to see black eyes in every direction regarding him with a thousand varying expressions of curiosity, indifference, sympathy, cheerfulness, sadness, and drowsiness.

The same day I went to see the Museum of Painting. The Seville gallery does not contain very many paintings, but those few are worth a great museum. There are the masterpieces of Murillo, and among them his immortal *Saint Anthony of Padua*, which is said to be the most divinely inspired of his works, and one of the greatest achieve-

ments of human genius. I visited the gallery
in the company of Señor Gonzalo Segovia and
Ardizone, one of the most illustrious young men
of Seville, and I wish he were here beside my table
at this moment to testify in a foot-note that when
my eyes first lit upon the picture I seized his arm
and uttered a cry.

Only once in my life have I felt such a profound
stirring of my soul as that which I felt on seeing
this picture. It was one beautiful summer night:
the sky was bright with stars, and the vast plain lay
extended before me from the high place where I
stood in deep silence. One of the noblest creatures
I have ever met in my life was at my side. A few
hours before we had been reading some pages from
one of Humboldt's works: we looked at the sky
and talked of the motion of the earth, the millions
of worlds, and the infinite with those suppressed
tones as of distant voices which one unconsciously
uses in speaking of such things in the silent night.
Finally we were still, and each, with eyes fixed on
the heavens, gave himself up to fancies. I know
not by what train of thought I was led; I know not
what mysterious chain of emotions was formed in
my heart; I know not what I saw or felt or dreamed.
I only know that suddenly a veil before my mind
seemed to be rent asunder; I felt within me a perfect assurance of that which hitherto I had longed
for rather than believed; my heart expanded with

a feeling of supreme joy, angelic peace, and limitless hope; a flood of scalding tears suddenly filled my eyes, and, grasping the hand of my friend, which sought my own, I cried from the depths of my soul, "It is true! It is true!" and began to cry like a child.

The *Saint Anthony of Padua* brought back the emotions of that evening. The saint is kneeling in the middle of his cell; the child Jesus in a nebulous halo of white vaporous light, drawn by the power of his prayer, is descending into his arms. Saint Anthony, rapt in ecstasy, throws himself forward with all his power of body and soul, his head thrown back, radiant with an expression of supreme joy. So great was the shock which this picture gave me that when I had looked at it a few moments I was as exhausted as if I had visited a vast gallery, and a trembling seized me and continued so long as I remained in that room.

Afterward I saw the other great paintings of Murillo—a *Conception*, a *Saint Francis embracing Christ*, another version of *Saint Anthony*, and others to the number of twenty or more, among them the famous and enchanting *Virgin of the Napkin*, painted by Murillo upon a real napkin in the Capuchin convent of Seville to gratify a desire of a lay brother who was serving him: it is one of his most delicate creations, in which is revealed all the magic of his inimitable coloring—but none of these paintings, although they are objects of wonder to all the artists of the world, drew my heart or thoughts from that divine *Saint Anthony.*

There are also in this gallery paintings by the two Herreras, Pacheco, Alonzo Cano, Pablo de Cespedes, Valdes, Mulato, a servant of Murillo who ably imitated his style, and finally the large famous painting of the *Apotheosis of Saint Thomas of Aquinas,* by Francesco Zurbaran, one of the most eminent artists of the seventeenth century, called the Spanish Caravaggio, and possibly his superior in truth and moral sentiment,—a powerful naturalist, a strong colorist, and an inimitable painter of austere friars, macerated saints, brooding hermits, and terrible priests, and an unsurpassed poet of penitence, solitude, and meditation.

After seeing the picture-gallery Señor Gonzalo Segovia led me through a succession of narrow streets to the street *Francos,* one of the principal ways of the city, and stopped me in front of a little draper's shop, saying with a laugh, " Look ! Doesn't this shop make you think of something ?"

" Nothing at all," I replied.

" Look at the number."

" It is number fifteen : what of it ?"

" Oh ! plague on it !" exclaimed my amiable guide,

> " ' Number fifteen,
>   On the left-hand side' !"

" The shop of the *Barber of Seville !*" I cried.

" Precisely !" he responded—"the shop of the Barber of Seville ; but be on your guard when you speak of it in Italy ; do not take your oath, for traditions are often misleading, and I would not assume the responsibility of confirming a fact of such importance."

At that moment the merchant came to the door of the shop, and, divining why we were there, laughed and said, " *No esta* " (" Figaro is not here "), and with a gracious bow he retired.

Then I besought Señor Gonzalo to show me a *patio*, one of those enchanting *patios* which as I looked at them from the street made me imagine so many delightful things. "I want to see at least one," I said to him—"to penetrate once into the midst of those mysteries, to touch the walls, to assure myself that it is a real thing and not a vision."

My desire was at once fulfilled : we entered the *patio* of one of his friends. Señor Gonzalo told the servant the object of our visit, and we were left alone. The house was only two stories in height. The *patio* was no larger than an ordinary room, but all marble and flowers, and a little fountain in the middle, and paintings and statues around, and from roof to roof an awning which sheltered it from the sun. In a corner was a work-table, and here and there one saw low chairs and little benches whereon a few moments previously had doubtless rested the feet of some fair Andalusian, who at that moment was watching us from between the slats of a blind.   I examined everything minutely, as I would have done in a house abandoned by the fairies: I sat down, closed my eyes, imagined I was the master, then arose, wet my hand with the spray of the fountain, touched a slender column, went to the door, picked a flower, raised my eyes to the windows, laughed, sighed, and said, " How happy must those be who live here !"   At that moment I heard a low laugh, and saw two great black eyes flash behind a blind and instantly disappear.   " Truly," I said, " I did not believe that it was possible to still live so poetically upon this earth.   And to think that you enjoy these houses all your life ! and that you have the inclination to rack your brains about politics !"

Señor Gonzalo showed me the secrets of the house.   " All this furniture," said he, " these paintings, and these vases of flowers disappear on the approach of autumn and are taken to the second story, which is the living apartment from autumn to spring.   When summer comes beds, wardrobes, tables, chairs—everything is brought down to the rooms on the ground floor, and here the family sleep and eat, receive their friends, and do their work, among the flowers and marbles to the murmur of the fountain.   And at night they have the doors open, and from the sleeping-rooms one can see the *patio* flooded with moonlight and smell the fragrance of roses."

"Oh, stop!" I exclaimed, "stop, Señor Gonzalo! Have pity on strangers!" And, laughing heartily, we both went out on our way to see the famous *Casa de Pilato.*

As we were passing along a lonely little street I looked in a window of a hardware-shop and saw an assortment· of knives so long, broad, and unusual that I felt a desire to buy one. I entered: twenty were displayed before my eyes, and I had the salesman to open them one by one. As each knife was opened I took a step backward. I do not believe it is possible to imagine an instrument more barbarous and terrifying in appearance than one of them. The handles are of wood, copper, and horn, curved and carved in open patterns, so that one may see through their little pieces of isinglass. The knives open with a sound like a rattle, and out comes a large blade as broad as the palm of your hand, as long as both palms together, and as sharp as a dagger, in the form of a fish, ornamented with red inlaying, which suggests streaks of clotted blood, and adorned with fierce and threatening inscriptions. On the blade of one there will be written in Spanish, *Do not open me without reason, nor shut me without honor;* on another, *Where I strike, all is over;* on a third, *When this snake bites, there is nothing left for the doctor to do;* and other gallantries of the same sort. The proper name of these knives is *na-vaja*—a word which also has the meaning of razor—and the *navaja* is the popular duelling weapon. Now it has fallen into disuse, but was at one time held in great honor; there were masters who taught its use, each of whom had his secret blow, and duels were fought in accordance with the rules of chivalry. I bought the most terrible *navaja* in the shop, and we entered the street again.

The *Casa de Pilato*, held by the Medina-Coeli family, is, after the Alcazar, the most beautiful monument of Moorish architecture in Seville. The name, *Casa de Pilato*, comes from the fact that its founder, Don Enriquez de Ribera, the first marquis of Tarifa, had it built, as the story goes, in imitation of the house of the Roman prætor, which he had seen in Jerusalem, where he went on a pilgrimage. The edifice has a modest exterior, but the interior is marvellous. One first enters a court not less beautiful than the enchanting court of the Alcazar, encircled by two orders of arches, supported by graceful marble columns, forming two very light galleries, one above the other, and so delicate that it seems as if the first puff of wind would cast them into ruins. In the centre is a lovely fountain resting on four marble dolphins and crowned by a bust of Janus. Around the lower part of the walls run brilliant mosaics, and above these every sort of fantastic arabesque, here and there framing beautiful niches

containing busts of the Roman emperors. At the
four corners of the court the ceilings, the walls, and
the doors are carved, embroidered, and covered
with flowers and historic tapestries with the delicacy
of a miniature. In an old chapel, partly Moorish
and partly Gothic in style, and most delicate in form,
there is preserved a little column, scarcely more than
three feet in height, the gift of Pius V. to a descendant of the founder of the palace, at one time viceroy
of Naples: to that column, says the tradition, was
bound Jesus of Nazareth to be scourged. This fact,
even if it were true, would prove that Pius V. did
not believe it in the slightest degree. For he would
not lightly have committed the unpardonable mistake
of depriving himself of a valuable relic to make a
present to the first comer. The entire palace is full
of sacred memories. On the first floor the custodian
points out a window which corresponds to that by
which Peter sat when he denied his Lord, and the
little window from which the maid-servant recognized him. From the street one sees another window with a little stone balcony, which represents the
exact position of the window where Jesus, wearing
the crown of thorns, was shown to the people.

The garden is full of fragments of ancient statuary
brought from Italy by that same Don Pedro Afan de
Ribera, viceroy of Naples. Among the other fables
that are told about this mysterious garden is one to
the effect that Don Pedro Afan de Ribera placed in

it an urn brought from Italy containing the ashes
of the emperor Trajan, and a curious person care-
lessly struck the urn and overturned it; the emperor's ashes were thus scattered over the grass, and
no one has ever succeeded in collecting them. So this
august monarch, born at Italica, by a very strange
fate has returned to the vicinity of his natal city,
not in the very best condition in which to meditate
upon its ruins, to tell the truth, but he was near it,
at any rate.

In spite of all that I have described, I may say
that I did not see Seville, but just commenced to see
it. Nevertheless, I shall stop here, because everything must have an end. I pass by the promenaders,
the squares, the gates, the libraries, the public buildings, the mansions of the grandees, the gardens and
the churches; but allow me to say that, after several
days' wandering through Seville from sunrise to sunset, I was obliged to leave the city under the weight
of a self-accusing conscience. I did not know which
way to turn. I had reached such a condition of
weariness that the announcement of a new object to
be seen filled me with foreboding rather than pleasure. The good Señor Gonzalo kept up my courage,
comforted me, and shortened the journeys with his
delightful company, but, nevertheless, I have only a
very confused remembrance of all that I saw during
those last days.

Seville, although it no longer merits the glorious

title of the Spanish Athens, as in the times of
Charles V. and Philip II., when it was mother and
patron of a large and chosen band of poets and
artists, the seat of culture and of the arts in the vast
empire of its monarchs, is even yet that one among
the cities of Spain, with the exception of Madrid, in
which the artistic life is most vigorously maintained,
as is evidenced by the number of its men of genius,
the liberality of its patrons, and the popular love of
the fine arts. It contains a flourishing academy of
literature, a society for the protection of the arts, a
well-known university, and a colony of scholars and
sculptors who enjoy an honorable distinction throughout Spain. But the highest literary fame in Seville
belongs to a woman—Catharine Bohl, the author of
the novels which bear the name of Fernan Caballero,
widely read in Spain and America, translated into
almost all the languages of Europe, and known also
in Italy (where some of them were published not
long since) by every one who at all occupies himself
with foreign literature. They are admirable pictures
of Andalusian manners, full of truth, passion, and
grace, and, above all, possessing a vigor of faith and
a religious enthusiasm so fearless and a Christian
charity so broad that they would startle and confuse
the most skeptical man in the world. Catharine
Bohl is a woman who would undergo martyrdom
with the firmness and serenity of a Saint Ignatius.
The consciousness of her power is revealed in every

page : she does not hesitate to defend her religion, and confronts, assails, threatens, and overthrows its enemies; and not only the enemies of religion, but every man and everything that, to use a common expression, conforms to the spirit of the age, for she never forgives the least sin which has been committed from the times of the Inquisition to our own day, and she is more inexorable than the Pope's syllabus.   And herein perhaps lies her greatest defect as a writer—that her religious convictions and her invectives are entirely too frequent and grow tiresome, and disgust and prejudice the reader rather than convince him of her own beliefs.   But there is not a shadow of bitterness in her heart, and as her books, so is her life, noble, upright, and charitable. In Seville she is revered as a saint.   Born in that city, she married early in life, and is now a widow for the third time.   Her last husband, who was Spanish ambassador at London, committed suicide, and from that day she has never laid aside her mourning.   At the time of my visit she was almost seventy ; she had been very beautiful, and her noble, placid face still preserved the impress of beauty. Her father, who was a man of considerable genius and great culture, taught her several languages in early life : she knows Latin thoroughly and speaks Italian, German, and French with admirable facility. At this time, however, she is not writing at all, although the editors and publishers of Europe and

America are offering her large sums for her works.
But she does not live a life of inactivity. From
morning to night she reads all sorts of books, and
while she reads she is either knitting or embroider-
ing, for she very firmly believes that her literary
studies ought not to take one minute from her feminine employments. She has no children, and lives
in a lonely house, the best part of which has been
given to a poor family; she spends a great part of
her income in charity. A curious trait of her character is her great love of animals: she has her
house full of birds, cats, and dogs, and her sensi-
bilities are so delicate that she has never consented
to enter a carriage, for fear of seeing the horse beaten
on her account. All suffering affects her as if she
herself were bearing it: the sight of a blind man or
of a sick person or of a cripple of any sort distresses
her for an entire day; she cannot close her eyes to
sleep unless she has wiped away a tear; she would
joyfully forego all her honors to save any unknown
person a heartache. Before the Revolution her life
was not so isolated: the Montpensier family received
her with great honor, and the most illustrious families of Seville vied with each other in entertaining
her at their homes: now she lives only among her
books and a few friends.

In Moorish times Cordova took the lead in literature and Seville in music. "When a scholar dies
at Seville," said Averroes, "and they wish to sell

his books, they send them to Cordova; but if a
musician dies at Cordova, they send his instruments
to Seville to be sold." Now Cordova has lost her
literary primacy, and Seville holds first place both
in literature and music. Truly the times are past
in which a poet by singing of the beauty of a maiden
draws around her a crowd of lovers from all parts
of the realm, and when one prince envies another
simply because a poet has sung in his praise a verse
more beautiful than any which the other had inspired, and a caliph rewards the author of a noble
hymn by a gift of a hundred camels, a troop of
slaves, and a vase of gold—when a happy strophe
improvised at an opportune time releases a slave
from his chains or saves the life of one condemned
to death, and when the musicians are followed
through the streets of Seville by a train of monarchs,
and the favor of poets is more sought than that of
kings, and the lyre is more terrible than the sword.
But the people of Seville are always the most poetic
people of Spain. The *bon mot*, the word of love,
the expression of joy and enthusiasm, fly from their
lips with a fascinating spontaneity and grace. The
common people of Seville improvise, and talk as
though they are singing, gesticulate as if they are
declaiming, laugh and play like children. One
never grows old at Seville. It is a city where life
melts away in a continuous smile, with no other
thought than the enjoyment of the beautiful sky,

the lovely little houses, and the delightful little gardens. It is the most peaceful city in Spain, and the only one which since the Revolution has not been agitated by those sad political commotions which have stirred the others: politics do not penetrate the surface; the Sevillians are content to make love; all else they take in jest. *Todo lo toman de broma*, say the other Spaniards of the Sevillians; and in truth with that fragrant air, with those little streets like those of an Oriental city, with those fiery little women, why should they trouble themselves? At Madrid they speak ill of them; they say they are vain, false, fickle, and silly. It is jealousy: they envy them their happy indolence, the sympathy which they inspire in strangers, their girls, their poets, their painters, their orators, their Giralda, their Alcazar, their Guadalquivir, their life, and their history. So say the Sevillians, striking their breasts with one hand and puffing into the air a cloud of smoke from the inseparable *cigaritto*; and their lovely little women 'revenge themselves upon their envious sisters and all the other women in the world, speaking with spiteful pity of long feet, large waists, and dull eyes, that in Andalusia would not receive the honor of a glance or the homage of a sigh. A charming and amiable people, in truth; but, alas! one must look at the reverse side of the medal: superstition reigns and schools are lacking, as is the case throughout all Southern Spain; this is partly their own fault and partly not; but the negative is probably the smaller part.

The day of my departure arrived unexpectedly. It is strange: I remember scarcely any particulars of my life at Seville; it is remarkable if I can tell where I dined, what I talked about with the consul, how I spent the evenings, and why I chose any given day to take my departure. I was not myself; I lived, if I may use the expression, out of myself; all the while I remained in the city I was a little dazed. Apart from the art-gallery and the *patio* my friend Segovia must have found that I knew very little; and now, I know not why, I think of those days as of a dream. Of no other city are my recollections so vague as of Seville. Even to-day, while I am certain of having been at Saragossa, Madrid, and Toledo, sometimes when I think of Seville a doubt steals upon me. It seems to me like a city much farther away than the most distant boundaries of Spain, and that to journey there again I must travel months and months, cross unknown continents and wide seas, among people totally different from our own. I think of the streets of Seville, of certain little squares and certain houses, as I would think of the spots on the moon. Sometimes the image of that city passes before my eyes like a white figure, and disappears almost before I can grasp it with my mind—sometimes in a breath of air, at certain hours of the day, at a garden-gate; in humming a song which I heard a boy sing on the steps of the Giralda. I cannot explain this secret to myself; I think of Seville as of a city which I have still to see, and I enjoy looking at the prints and thumbing the books which I bought there, for they are tangible things that convince me of my visit. A month ago I received a letter from Segovia which said, "Come back to us." It gave me untold pleasure, but at the same time I laughed as if he had written, "Make a voyage to Pekin." It is for this very reason that Seville is dearer to me than all the other cities of Spain; I love it as I might love a beautiful unknown woman who, crossing a mysterious wood, might look my way and throw me a flower. How often in the theatre or at the café, when a friend shakes me and asks, "What are you thinking about?" I am obliged to leave the little room of Maria de Padilla to return to him, or a boat that is gliding along in the shade of the Christina plane trees, or Figaro's shop, or the vestibule of a *patio* full of flowers, fountains, and lights.

I embarked on a boat of the Segovia Company, near the Torre del Oro, at an hour when Seville is wrapped in deep sleep and a burning sun covers it with a flood of light. I remember that a few moments before the boat started a young man came on board in search of me, and gave me a letter from Gonzalo Segovia, containing a sonnet which I still cherish as one of my most precious mementos of

Seville.   On the boat there was a company of Spanish singers, an English family, some laboring-men,
and babies.   The captain, being a good Andalusian,
had a cheery word for everybody.   I soon began a
conversation with him.   My friend Gonzalo was a
son of the proprietor of the line, and we talked of
the Segovia family, of Seville, the sea, and a thousand pleasant things.   Ah! the poor man was far
from thinking that a few days later the unlucky ship
would founder in the midst of the sea and bring him
to such a terrible end!   It was the *Guadaira*, that
was lost a short distance from Marseilles by the
bursting of the boiler on the sixteenth day of June,
1872.

At three o'clock the boat started for Cadiz.

CADIZ.

CADIZ.

THAT was the most delightful evening of all my journey.

A little while after the ship had commenced to move there sprang up one of those gentle breezes which played with one as an infant plays with one's cravat or a lock of one's hair, and from stem to stern there was a sound of the voices of women and children, like that which one hears among a group of friends at the first crack of the whip announcing their departure for a merry outing. All the passengers gathered at the stern in the shade of a gayly-colored awning like a Chinese pavilion: some were sitting on coils of rope, others were stretched at full length on the benches, others were leaning against the rail—every one looked back in the direction of the Torre del Oro to enjoy the famous and enchanting spectacle of Seville as it faded away in the distance. Some of the women had not yet dried the tears of parting, and some of the children were still a little frightened by the sound of the engine. And some ladies were still quarrelling with the porters for abusing their baggage; but in a few moments all was serene again, and the passengers began to

149

peel oranges, light cigars, pass little flasks of liquor, converse with their unknown neighbors, sing and laugh, and in a quarter of an hour we were all friends.

The boat glided along as smoothly as a gondola over the still, limpid waters, which reflected the white dresses of the ladies like a mirror, and the breeze brought the delightful fragrance from the orange-groves of the villas scattered along the shore. Seville was hidden behind her circle of gardens, and we saw only an immense mass of trees of vivid green, and above them the black pile of the cathedral and the rose-colored Giralda surmounted by its statue flaming like a tongue of fire. As the distance widened the cathedral appeared grander and more majestic, as if it were following the vessel and gaining upon her: now, although still following, it seemed to retire a great way from the shore; now it would seem to be spanning the river; one moment it would appear suddenly to return to its place; a moment later it looked so close that we suspected the boat had turned back. The Guadalquivir wound along in short curves, and as the boat turned this way and that Seville appeared and disappeared, now peeping out in one place as if it had stolen beyond its boundaries, now raising its head suddenly behind a wood, gleaming like a snow-clad mountain, now revealing some white streaks here and there amid the verdure, and suddenly disappearing from view and performing all sorts of fantastic wiles, like a coquettish woman. Finally it disappeared and we saw it no more : the cathedral alone remained. Then every one turned to look at the shore. We seemed to be sailing on the lake of a garden. Here was a hillside clothed with cypresses, here a hilltop all covered with flowers, yonder a village extending along the shore, and under the garden trellises and along the terraces of the villas sat ladies look-ing at us with spy-glasses; and here and there were peasants' families in brightly-colored dresses, sail-boats; and naked boys who plunged into the water and turned sommersaults, frisked about, shouted, and waved their hands toward the ladies on the boat, who covered their faces with their fans. Some miles from Seville we met three steamboats, one after the other. The first came upon us so sud-denly at a turn of the river that, having had no experience in that sort of navigation, I was afraid, for a moment, that we should not have time to avoid a collision; the two boats almost grazed each other in passing, and the passengers of each saluted each other and threw across oranges and cigars, and charged each other with messages to be borne to Cadiz or Seville.

My fellow-voyagers were almost all Andalusians, and so, after an hour of conversation, I knew them from first to last as well as if we had all been friends from infancy. Every one instantly told every one else, whether he wanted to know it or not, who he was, his age, occupation, and where he was going, and one even went so far as to tell how many sweethearts he had and how many pesetas were in his purse. I was taken for a singer; and this is not strange if one considers that in Spain the people think three-fourths of the Italians are trained to sing, dance, or declaim. One .gentleman, noticing that I had an Italian book in my hand, asked me, point-blank, "Where did you leave the company ?"

"What company ?" I demanded.

"Weren't you singing with Fricci at the Zarzuela ?"

"I am sorry, but I have never appeared on the stage."

"Well, I must say, then, that you and the second tenor look as much alike as two drops of water."

"You don't say so ?"

"Pray excuse me."

"It's of no consequence."

"But you are an Italian ?"

"Yes."

"Do you sing ?"

"I am sorry, but I do not sing."

"How strange! To judge by your throat and breast, I should have said that you must have a splendid tenor voice."

I put my hand to my chest and neck, and replied, "It may be so; I will try—one never knows. I have two of the necessary qualifications: I am an Italian and have the throat of a tenor; the voice ought to follow."

At this point the prima donna of the company, who had overheard the dialogue, entered the conversation, and after her the entire company:

"Is the gentleman an Italian?"

"At your service, madam."

"I ask the question because I wish him to do me a favor. What is the meaning of those short verses from *Il Trovatore* which run—

"Non può nemmeno un Dio
Donna rapirti a me."
(Not even a god can steal my lady from me.)

"Is the lady married?"

They all began to laugh.

"Yes," replied the prima donna; "but why do you ask me that?"

"Because . . . 'not even a god can steal you from me' is what your husband ought to say, if he has two good eyes in his head, every morning when he rises and every night when he goes to bed."

The others laughed, but to the prima donna this imaginary presumption on the part of her husband in affirming that he was secure even against a god seemed too extravagant, possibly because she knew that she had not always been sufficiently wary in her regard for men; and so she scarcely deigned by so

much as a smile to show that she had understood
my compliment.   She at once asked the meaning of
another verse, and after her the baritone, and after
the baritone the tenor, and after the tenor the second
lady, and so on, until for a little while I did nothing
but translate poor Italian verses into worse Spanish
prose, to the great satisfaction of some of them, who
for the first time were able to repeat intelligently a
little of what they had so often sung with an air of
perfect knowledge.   When every one had learned as
much as he wished to know, the conversation came
to a close, and I stood talking a little while with the
baritone, who hummed me an air from the *Zarzuela* ;
then I attached myself to one of the chorus, who
told me that the tenor was making love to the
prima donna; then I went off with the tenor, who
told me about the baritone's wife; then I talked
with the prima donna, who said disagreeable things
about the whole company ; but they were all good
friends, and when they met, as they walked about
the boat and gathered under the awning, the men
pulled each other's beards and the women kissed
each other, and one and all exchanged glances and
smiles which revealed secret understandings.   Some
ran through the gamut here, some hummed yonder,
others practised trills in a corner, and others again
tried a gutteral *do* that ended in a wheezing sound
in the throat ; and meanwhile they all talked at once
about a thousand trifles.

Finally, the bell sounded and we rushed headlong to the table, like so many officials invited to a spread at the unveiling of a monument. At this dinner, amid the cries and songs of all those people, I drank for the first time an unmixed glass of that terrible wine of Xeres whose wonders are sung in the four corners of the earth. I had scarcely swallowed it before I seemed to feel a spark run through all my veins, and my head burned as if it was full of sulphur. All the others drank, and all were filled with unrestrained mirth and became irresistibly loquacious; the prima donna began to talk in Italian, the tenor in French, the baritone in Portuguese, the others in dialect, and I in every tongue; and there were toasts and snatches of song, shouts, arch glances, clasping of hands above table and the kicking of feet below, and declarations of good fellowship exchanged on all sides, like the personalities in Parliament when the opposing factions join battle. After dinner we all went on deck, flushed and in great spirits, breathless and enveloped in a cloud of smoke from our cigarettes, and then, in the light of the moon, whose silvery rays gleamed on the wide river and covered the hillsides and the groves with limpid light, we began again a noisy conversation, and after the conversation there was singing, not only the trifling airs of *Zarzuela,* but passages from operas, with solos, duets, trios, and choruses, with appropriate gestures and stage strides, diversified

with declamations from the poets, stories, and anecdotes, hearty laughter, and tumultuous applause;
finally, tired and breathless, we were all silent, and
some fell asleep with upturned faces, others went to
lie down under cover, and the prima donna seated
herself in a corner to look at the moon. The tenor
was snoring. I profited by the occasion to go and
have an aria from the *Zarzuela—El Sargento Fede-
rico*—sung to me in a low voice. The courteous
Andalusian did not wait to be pressed: she sang,
but suddenly she was silent and hid her face. I
looked at her: she was weeping. I asked her the
cause of her distress, and she answered, sadly, "I
am thinking of a perjury." Then she broke into
a laugh and began to sing again. She had a melo-
dious, flexible voice, and sang with a feeling of
gentle sadness. The sky was all studded with stars,
and the boat glided so smoothly through the water
that it scarcely seemed to be moving; and I thought
of the gardens of Seville, of the near African shore,
and of the dear one waiting for me in Italy, and my
eyes too were wet, and when the lady stopped singing, I said, "Sing on, for—

> 'Mortal tongue cannot express
> That which I felt within my breast. . . . ' "

At dawn the boat was just entering the ocean;
the river was very wide. The right bank, scarcely
visible in the distance, stretched along like a tongue

of land, beyond which shone the waters of the sea. A moment later the sun rose above the horizon, and the vessel left the river. Then there unfolded before my eyes a sight that could not be described if it were possible to join poetry, painting, and music in one supreme art—a spectacle whose magnificence and enchantment I believe not even Dante could describe with his grandest images, nor Titian with his most brilliant colors, nor Rossini with his most perfect harmonies, nor even all three of them together. The sky was a miracle of sapphire light unflecked by a cloud, and the sea was so beautiful that it seemed like an immense carpet of shimmering silk; the sun was shining on the crests of the little ripples caused by a light breeze, and it seemed as if they were tipped with amethyst. The sea was full of reflections and luminous bands of light, and in the distance were streaks of silver, with here and there great white sails, like the trailing wings of gigantic fallen angels. I have never seen such brilliancy of color, such splendor of light, such freshness, such transparancy, such limpid water and sky. It seemed like a daybreak of creation, which the fancy of poets had pictured so pure and effulgent that our dawns are only pale reflections in comparison. It was more than Nature's awakening and the recurring stir of life: it was a hallelujah, a triumph, a new birth of creation, growing into the infinite by a second inspiration of God.

I went below deck to get my spyglass, and when
I returned Cadiz was in sight.

The first impression which it made upon me was
a feeling of doubt whether it was a city or not. I
first laughed, then turned toward my fellow-traveller
with the air of one seeking to be assured that he is
not deceived. Cadiz is like an island of chalk. It
is a great white spot in the midst of the sea, without
a cloud, without a black line, without a shadow—a
white spot as clear and pure as a hilltop covered
with untrodden snow, standing out against a sky of
beryl and turquoise in the midst of a vast flooded
plain. A long, narrow neck of land unites it to the
continent; on all other sides it is surrounded by the
sea, like a boat just ready to sail bound to the shore
only by a cable. As we approached, the forms of
the campaniles, the outlines of the houses, and the
openings of the streets became clear, and everything
seemed whiter, and, however much I looked through
my spy-glass, I could not have discovered the
smallest spot in that whiteness, either on a building near the harbor or in the farthest suburbs. We
entered the port, where there were but a few ships
and those a great way apart. I stepped into a boat
without even taking my valise with me, for I was
obliged to leave for Malaga that same evening, and
so eager was I to see the city that when the boat
came to the bank, I jumped too soon and fell to the

ground like a corpse, although, alas! I still felt the
pains of a living body.

Cadiz is the whitest city in the world; and it is
of no use to contradict me by saying that I have
not seen every other city, for my common sense
tells me that a city whiter than this, which is super-
latively and perfectly white, cannot exist. Cordova and Seville cannot be compared with Cadiz:
they are as white as a sheet, but Cadiz is as white
as milk. To give an idea of it, one could not do
better than to write the word "white" a thousand
times with a white pencil on blue paper, and make
a note on the margin: "Impressions of Cadiz."
Cadiz is one of the most extravagant and graceful
of human caprices: not only the outer walls of the
houses are white, but the stairs are white, the courts
are white, the shop-walls are white, the stones are
white, the pilasters are white, the most secret and
darkest corners of the poorest houses and the lone-
liest streets are white; everything is white from
roof to cellar wherever the tip of a brush can enter,
even to the holes, cracks, and birds' nests. In every
house there is a pile of chalk and lime, and every
time the eagle eye of the inmates spies the least
spot the brush is seized and the spot covered.
Servants are not taken into families unless they
know how to whitewash. A pencil-scratch on a
wall is a scandalous thing, an outrage upon the
public peace, an act of vandalism: you might walk

through the entire city, look behind all the doors, and poke your nose into the very holes, and you would find white, only and always and eternally.

But, for all this, Cadiz does not in the least resemble the other Andalusian cities. Its streets are long and straight, and the houses are high, and lack the *patios* of Cordova and Seville. But, although the appearance is different, the city does not appear less interesting and pleasant to the eye of the stranger. The streets are straight, but narrow, and, moreover, they are very long, and many of them cross the entire city, and so one can see at the end, as through the crack in a door, a slender strip of sky, which makes it seem as if the city was built on the summit of a mountain cut on all sides in regular channels: moreover, the houses have a great many windows, and, as at Burgos, every window is provided with a sort of glass balcony which rises in tiers from story to story, so that in many streets the houses are completely covered with glass, and one sees scarcely any traces of the walls. It seems like walking through a passage in an immense museum. Here and there, between one house and the next, rise the graceful fronds of a palm; in every square there is a luxuriant mass of verdure, and at all the windows bunches of grass and bouquets of flowers.

Really, I had been far from imagining that Cadiz could be so gay and smiling—that terrible, ill-fated Cadiz, burned by the English in the sixteenth century, bombarded at the end of the eighteenth, devastated by the pestilence, hostess of the fleets of Trafalgar, the-seat of the revolutionary council during the War of Independence, the theatre of the horrible butchery of the Revolution of 1820, the target of the French bombs in 1823, the standard-bearer of the Revolution which hurled the Bourbons from the throne,—Cadiz always restless and turbulent and first of all to raise the battle-cry. But of such calamities and such struggles there remain only some cannon-balls half buried in the walls, for over all the traces of destruction has passed the inexorable brush, covering every dishonor with a white veil. And as it is with the latest wars, so too there remains not a trace of the Phœnicians who founded the city, nor of the Carthaginians and Romans who enlarged and beautified it, unless one wishes to consider as a trace the tradition which says, " Here rose a temple to Hercules," " There rose a temple to Saturn." But time has done a worse thing than to deprive Cadiz of her ancient monuments: it has stolen away her commerce and her riches since Spain lost her possessions in America, and now Cadiz lies there inert on her solitary rock, waiting in vain for the thousand ships which once came with flags and festoons to offer her the tribute of the New World.

I had a letter of introduction to the Italian consul, and after receiving it he courteously took me to the

top of a tower from which I was able to get a bird's-
eye view of the city. It was a novel sight and a
very lively surprise: seen from above, Cadiz is
white, entirely and perfectly white, just as it appears from the sea; there is not a roof in all the
city; every house is covered on top by a terrace
surrounded by a low whitewashed wall; on almost
every terrace rises a little white tower, which is surmounted, in its turn, by another smaller terrace or
by a little cupola or sort of sentry-box: everything
is white; all these little cupolas, these pinnacles,
and these towers, which give the city a very odd
and uneven appearance, gleam and stand out white
against the vivid blue of the sea. One's view extends over the entire length of the isthmus which
connects Cadiz to the main land, embraces a far-
off strip of distant coast whitened by the cities of
Puerto Real and Puerto Santa Maria, dotted with villages, churches, and villas, and includes also the port
and the clear and a very beautiful sky which vies
with the sea in transparency and light. I could not
look enough at that strange city. On closing my
eyes it appeared as if covered by an immense sheet.
Every house seemed to have been built for an as-
tronomical observatory. The entire population, in
case the sea should inundate the city, as in ancient
times, might gather on the terraces and remain there
in perfect ease, saving the fright.

I was told that a few years ago, on the occasion

of some eclipse of the sun, this very spectacle was witnessed: the seventy thousand inhabitants of Cadiz all ascended to the terraces to watch the phenomenon. The city changed its perfect whiteness for a thousand colors; every terrace was thick with heads; one saw at a single glance, quarter after quarter, and finally the entire population: a low murmur rose to heaven like the roar of the sea, and a great movement of arms, fans, and spy-glasses, pointing upward, made it seem as if the people were awaiting the descent of some angel from the solar sphere. At a certain moment there was a profound silence: when the phenomenon was over the entire population gave a shout, which sounded like a clap of thunder, and a few moments later the city was white again.

I descended from the tower and went to see the cathedral, a vast marble edifice of the sixteenth century, not to be compared to the cathedrals of Burgos and Toledo, but nevertheless dignified and bold in architecture and enriched by every sort of treasure, like all the other Spanish churches. I went to see the convent where Murillo was painting a picture over a high altar when he fell from the scaffold and received the wound which caused his death. I passed through the picture-gallery, which contains some fine paintings of Zurbaran; entered the bull-ring, built entirely of wood, which was created in a few days to provide a spectacle for Queen Isabella. Toward evening I took a turn in the delightful promenade along the sea-shore, in the midst of orange trees and palms, where the most beautiful and elegant ladies of the city were pointed out to me, one by one. Whatever may be the judgment of the Spaniards, to me the feminine type of Cadiz did not seem at all inferior to the celebrated type of Seville. The women are a little taller, a little heavier, and are somewhat darker. Some observer has ventured to say that they closely resemble the Grecian type, but I do not know in what respect. I saw no difference from the Andalusian type except in stature, and that was enough to make me heave sighs which might have propelled a ship, and constrained me to return as soon as possible to the vessel as a place of refuge and peace.

When I arrived on board it was night; the sky was all twinkling with stars, and the breeze bore faintly to my ears the music of a band playing on the promenade of Cadiz. The singers were asleep; I was alone, and the sight of the city lights and the recollection of the lovely faces filled me with melancholy. I did not know what to do with myself, so I went down to the cabin, took out my note-book, and commenced the description of Cadiz. But I only succeeded in writing ten times the words, "White, blue, snow, brightness, colors," after which I made a little sketch of a woman and then closed my eyes and dreamed of Italy.

MALAGA.

MALAGA.

THE next day, at sunset, the vessel was passing through the Straits of Gibraltar.

Now, as I look at that point on the map, it seems so near home that when I am in the humor and my domestic finances permit I ought not to hesitate a moment to pack my valise and run down to Genoa on my way to enjoy a second time the most beautiful sight of two continents. But then it seemed to be so far away that when I had written a letter to my mother on the rail of the ship, intending to give it to one of the passengers for Gibraltar to post, as I was writing the address I laughed at my confidence, as if it were impossible for a letter to travel all the way to Turin. "From here!" I thought—"from the Pillars of Hercules!" and I pronounced the Pillars of Hercules as if I had said the Cape of Good Hope or Japan.

". . . I am on the ship Guadaira: behind me is the ocean, and in front the Mediterranean, on the left Europe and on the right Africa. On this side I see the cape of Tarifa, and on that the mountains of the African coast, which look indistinct like a

167

gray cloud; I see Ceuta, and a little beyond it
Tangiers like a white spot, and in a direct line with
the ship rises the Rock of Gibraltar. The sea is as
placid as a lake, and the sky is red and gold; all is
serene, beautiful, and magnificent, and I feel in my
mind an inexpressible and delightful stirring of
great thoughts, which, if I could put them into
words, would become a joyful prayer beginning and
ending with thy name. . . ."

The vessel stopped in the Gulf of Algeciras: the
entire company of singers got into a large boat
from Gibraltar, and went off, waving fans and hand-
kerchiefs as a parting salute. It was growing dark
when the boat started again. Then I was able to
measure the enormous mass of the Rock of Gibraltar at every turn. At first I thought we should leave
it behind in a few moments, but the moments became
hours. Gradually, as we approached, it towered
above us, and presented a new appearance every instant—now the silhouette of some measureless monster, now the image of an immense staircase, now
the outline of a fantastic castle, now a shapeless
mass like a monstrous aërolite fallen from a world
shivered in a battle of the spheres. Then, on nearer
view, behind a high rock like an Egyptian pyramid,
there came into sight a great projection as large as
a mountain, with fissures and broken boulders and
vast curves which lost themselves in the plain. It
was night; the rock stood outlined against the moon-

lit sky as clear and sharp as a sheet of black paper on a pane of glass. One saw the lighted windows of the English barracks, the sentry-boxes on the summit of the dizzy crags, and a dim outline of trees which seemed little larger than a tuft of grass among the nearest rocks. For a long time the boat seemed motionless or else the rock was receding, so close and threatening did it always appear; then, little by little, it began to diminish, but our eyes were weary of gazing before the rock grew weary of threatening us with its fantastic transformations. At midnight I gave a final salute to that formidable, lifeless sentinel of Europe, and went to wrap myself up in my little corner.

At break of day I awoke a few miles from the port of Malaga.

The city of Malaga, seen from the port, presents a pleasing appearance not wholly without grandeur. On the right is a high rocky mountain, upon the top of which and down one side, even to the plain, are the enormous blackened ruins of the castle of Gibralfaro, and on the lower slopes stands the cathedral towering majestically above all the surrounding buildings, lifting toward heaven, as an inspired poet might say, two beautiful towers and a very high belfry. Between the castle and the church and on the face and sides of the mountain there is a mass —a *canaille*, as Victor Hugo would say—of smoky little houses, placed confusedly one above the other,

as if they had been thrown down from above like
stones. To the left of the cathedral, along the shore,
is a row of houses, gray, violet, or pale yellow in
color, with white window- and door-frames, that
suggest the villages along the Ligurian Riviera.
Beyond rises a circle of green and reddish hills enclosing the city like the walls of an amphitheatre,
and to the right and left along the sea-shore extend
other mountains, hills, and rocks as far as the eye
can see. The port was almost deserted, the shore
silent, and the sky very blue.

Before landing I took my leave of the captain,
who was going on to Marseilles, said good-bye to
the boatswain and passengers, telling them all that I
should arrive at Valencia a day ahead of the boat,
and I should certainly join them again and go on to
Barcelona and Marseilles, and the captain replied,
"We shall look for you," and the steward promised
that my place should be saved for me. How often
since then have I remembered the last words of those
poor people!

I stopped at Malaga with the intention of leaving
that same evening for Granada. The city itself
offers nothing worthy of note, excepting the new
part, which occupies a tract of land formerly
covered by the sea. This is built up in the modern
style, with wide, straight streets and large, bare
houses. The rest of the city is a labyrinth of narrow, winding streets and a mass of houses without

color, without *patios*, and without grace. There are some spacious squares with gardens and fountains; columns and arches of Moorish buildings, no modern monuments; a great deal of dirt, and not a great many people. The environs are very beautiful, and the climate is milder than that of Seville.

I had a friend at Malaga, and after finding him we passed the day together. He told me a curious fact: At Malaga there is a literary academy of more than eight hundred members, where they celebrate the birthdays of all the great writers, and hold twice a week a public lecture on some subject connected with literature or science. That same evening they were to celebrate a solemn function. Some months earlier the academy had offered a prize of three golden flowers, enamelled in different colors, to the three poets who should compose the best ode on "Progress," the best ballad on the "Recovery of Malaga," and the best satire on one of the most prevalent vices of modern society. The invitation had been extended to all the poets of Spain; poems had poured in in abundance; a board of judges had secretly considered them; and that very evening the choice was to be announced. The ceremony was to be conducted with great pomp. The bishop, the governor, the admiral, the most conspicuous personages of the city, with dress-coats, orders, and shoulder-scarfs, and a great number of ladies in evening dress, were to be present. The three most beautiful Muses

of the city were to present themselves on a sort of
stage adorned with garlands and flags, each of whom
was to open the roll containing the prize poem and
to proclaim three times the name of its author: if
the author were present, he was to be invited to read
his verses and receive his flower; if he were not
present, his verses were to be read for him.
Throughout the whole city they talked of nothing
but the academy, guessed the names of the victors,
predicted the wonders of the three poems, and extolled the decorations of the hall.   This festival of
poetry, called the *juegos floreales*, had not been celebrated for ten years.   Others may judge whether
such contests and displays benefit or injure poets
and poetry.   As for me, whatever may be the
dubious and fleeting literary glory which is bestowed
by the sentence of the jury and the homage of a
bishop and a governor, I believe that to receive
the gift of a golden flower from the hand of a most
beautiful woman under the eyes of five hundred fair
Andalusians, to the sound of soft music and amid
the perfume of jessamine and roses, that would be
a delight even truer and more lively than any which
comes from real and enduring glory.   No? Ah! we
are sincere.

One of my first thoughts was to taste a little of
the genuine Malaga wine, for no other reason than
to repay myself for the many headaches and stomach-
aches caused by the miserable concoctions sold in

many Italian cities under the false recommendation
of its name. But either I did not know how to ask
or they did not wish to understand: the fact remains
that the wine they gave me at the hotel burned my
throat and made my head spin. I was not able to
walk straight even to the cathedral, or from the
cathedral to the castle of Gibralfaro, or to the other
places, nor could I form an idea of the beauties of
Malaga without seeing them double and unsteadily,
as some spiteful person might suppose.

On our walk my friend talked to me about the
famous Republican people of Malaga, who are every
moment doing something on their own account.
They are a very fiery people, but fickle and yet
tractable, like all people who feel much and think
little; and they act upon the impulse of passion
rather than the strength of conviction. The least
trifle calls together an immense crowd and stirs up a
tumult that turns the city topsy-turvy; but on most
occasions a resolute act of a man in authority, an
exhibition of courage, or a burst of eloquence is
sufficient to quiet the tumult and disperse the crowd.
The nature of the people is good on the whole, but
superstition and passion have perverted them. And,
above all, superstition is perhaps more firmly en-
trenched in Malaga than in any other city of Andalusia, by reason of the greater popular ignorance.
Altogether, Malaga was the least Andalusian of the
cities I had seen: even the very language has been

corrupted, and they speak worse Spanish than at
Cadiz, where, forsooth! they speak badly enough.

I was still at Malaga, but my imagination was far
away among the streets of Granada and in the gardens of the Alhambra and the Generalife. Shortly
after the noon hour I took my leave from the only
city in Spain, to tell the truth, that I left without a
sigh of regret. When the train started, instead of
turning for a last look, as I had done in all of its
sister towns, I murmured the verses sung by Giovanni
Prati at Granada when the duke d'Aosta was leaving
for Spain:

"Non più Granata è sola
Sulle sur mute pietre;
L'inno in Alhambra vola
Sulle Moresche cetre."

(*No more does Granada stand alone on her silent
stones: the hymn flies to the Alhambra on Moorish
lyres.*)

And now, as I write them again, it seems to me
that the music of the band of the National Guard of
Turin inspires peace and gladness more even surely
than Moorish lyres, and that the pavement of the
porticoes of the Po, although it be ever so silent, is
better laid and smoother than the stones of Granada.

GRANADA.

GRANADA.

THE journey from Malaga to Granada was the most adventurous and unfortunate that I made in Spain.

In order that my compassionate readers may pity me as much as I desire, they must know (I am ashamed to occupy people with these little details) that at Malaga I had eaten only the lightest sort of an Andalusian repast, of which at the moment of departure I retained a very vague recollection. But I started, feeling sure that I could alight at some railway-station where there would be one of those rooms or public choking-places where one enters at a gallop, eats until one is out of breath, pays as one scampers out to rush into a crowded carriage, suffocated and robbed, to curse the sebedule, travel, and the minister of public works who deceives the country. I departed, and for the first hours it was delightful. The country was all gently sloping hills and green fields, dotted with villages crowned with palms and cypresses, and in the carriage, between two old men who rode with their eyes shut, there was a little Andalusian who kept looking around with a roguish smile which seemed to say, "Go on; your lovelorn glances do not offend me." But the train crept along as slowly as a worn-out diligence, and we stopped only a few moments at the stations. By sunset my stomach began to cry for help, and, to render the pangs of hunger even more severe, I was obliged to make a good part of the journey on foot. The train stopped at an unsafe bridge, and all the passengers got out and filed around, two by two, to meet the train on the other side of the river. We were surrounded by the rocks of the Sierra Nevada, in a wild, desert place, which made it seem as if we were a company of hostages led by a band of brigands. When we had clambered into the carriage the train crawled along no faster than before, and my stomach began to complain more desperately than at first. After a long time we arrived at a station all crowded with trains, where a large part of the travellers hurried out before I could reach the step.

"Where are you going?" asked a railroad official, who had seen me alight.

"To dine," I replied.

"But aren't you going to Granada?"

"Yes."

"Then you won't have time; the train starts immediately."

"But the others have gone."

"You will see them come back on the run in a minute."

The freight-trains in front prevented me from seeing the station; I thought it was a great way off, and so stayed where I was. Two minutes passed, five, eight; the tourists did not return and the train did not start. I jumped out, ran to the station, saw a café, and entered a large room. Great heavens! Fifty starving people were standing around a refreshment-table with their noses in their plates, elbows in the air, and their eyes on the clock, devouring and shouting; another fifty were crowding around a counter seizing and pocketing bread, fruit, and candies, while the proprietor and the waiters, panting like horses and streaming with sweat, ran about, tucked up their sleeves, howled, tumbled over the seats and upset the customers, and scattered here and there streams of soup and drops of sauce; and one poor women, who must have been the mistress of the café, imprisoned in a little niche behind the besieged counter, ran her hands through her hair in desperation. At this sight my arms hung down helplessly. But suddenly I roused myself and made an onslaught. Driven back by a feminine elbow in my chest, I rushed in again; repulsed by a jab in the stomach, I gathered all my strength to make a third attack. At this point the bell rang. There was a burst of imprecations and then a falling of seats, a scattering of plates, a hurry-scurry, and a perfect pandemonium. One man, choking in the fury of his last mouthfuls, became livid and his eyes seemed bursting from his head as though he were being hanged; another in stretching out his hand to seize an orange, struck by some one rushing past, plunged it into a bowl of cream; another was running through the room in search of his valise with a great smear of sauce on his cheeks; another, who had tried to drink his wine at one gulp, had strangled and coughed as if he would tear open his stomach; the officials at the door cried, "Hurry!" and the travellers called back from the room, "Ahogate!" (choked), and the waiters ran after those who had not paid, and those who wanted to pay could not find the waiters; and the ladies swooned, and the children cried, and everything was upside down.

By good fortune I was able to get into my carriage before the train started.

But there a new punishment awaited me. The two old men and the little Andalusian, who must have been the daughter of the one and niece of the other, had been successful in securing a little booty in the midst of that accursed crowd at the counter, and they were eating right and left. I began to watch them with sorrowful eyes like a dog beside his master's table, counting the mouthfuls and the number of times they chewed. The little Andalusian noticed it, and, pointing to something which looked like a croquet, made a gracious bow as if to ask if I would take it.

"Oh no, thank you," I replied with the smile of a dying man; "I have eaten."

My angel, I continued to myself, if you only knew that at this moment I would prefer those two croquets to the bitter apples—as Sir Niccolo Machiavelli would generously say—even those bitter apples from the famous garden of the Hesperides!

"Try a drop of liquor at least," said the old uncle.

I do not know what childish pique against myself or against those good people took possession of me, but it was a feeling which other men experience on similar occasions; however, I replied this time too, "No, thank you; it would be bad for me."

The good old man looked me over from head to foot as if to say that I did not appear like a man to be the worse for a drop of liquor, and the Andalusian smiled, and I blushed for shame.

Night settled down, and the train went on at the pace of Sancho Panza's steed for I knew not how many hours. That night I felt for the first time in my life the pangs of hunger, which I thought I had felt already on the famous day of the twenty-fourth of June, 1866. To relieve these torments I obstinately thought of all the dishes which filled me with repugnance—raw tomatoes, snails in soup, roasted crabs, and snails in salad. Alas! a voice of derision told me, deep down in my vitals, that if I had any of them I should eat them and lick my fingers. Then I began to make imaginary messes of different dishes, as cream and fish, with a dash of wine, with a coat of pepper, and a layer of juniper preserves, to see if I could thus hold my stomach in check. Oh misery! my cowardly stomach did not repel even those. Then I made a final effort and imagined that I was at table in a Parisian hotel at the time of the siege, and that I gently lifted a mouse by the tail out of some pungent sauce, and the mouse, unexpectedly regaining life, bit my thumb and transfixed me with two wicked little eyes, and I, with raised fork, hesitated whether to let it go or to spit it without pity. But, thank Heaven! before I had settled this horrible question, to perform such an act as has never been recorded in the history of any siege, the train stopped and a ray of hope revived my drooping spirits.

We had reached some nameless village, and while I was putting my head out of the window a voice cried, " All out for Granada!" I rushed headlong from the carriage and found myself face to face with a huge bearded fellow, who took my valise, telling me that he was going to put it in the diligence, for from that village to I know not how many miles from *imperial Granada* there is no railway.

"One moment!" I cried to the unknown man in a supplicating voice: " how long before you start?"

"Two minutes," he replied.

"Is there an inn here?"

"There it is." I flew to the inn, bolted a hard-boiled egg, and rushed back to the diligence, crying, "How much time now?"

"Two minutes more," answered the same voice.

I flew back to the hotel, seized another egg, and ran again to the diligence with the question, "Are you off?"

"In a minute."

Back again to the inn, and a third egg, and then to the diligence: "Are we going?"

"In half a minute."

This time I heaved a mighty sigh, ran to the inn, swallowed a fourth egg and a glass of wine, and rushed toward the diligence. But before I had taken ten steps my breath gave out, and I stopped with the egg halfway down my throat. At this point the whip cracked.—"Wait!" I cried in a hoarse voice, waving my hands like a drowning man.

"*Que hay?*" (What's the matter?) demanded the driver.

I could not reply.

"He has an egg stuck in his throat," some stranger answered for me.

All the travellers burst into a laugh, the egg went down; I laughed too, overtook the diligence, which had already started, and, regaining my breath, gave

my companions an account of my troubles, and they
were much interested, and pitied me even more than
I had dared to hope after that cruel laugh at my
suffocation.

But my troubles were not ended.   One of those
irresistible attacks of sleepiness which used to come
upon me treacherously in the long night-marches
among the soldiers seized me all at once, and tor-
mented me as far as the railway-station without my
being able to get a moment of sleep.   I believe that
a cannon-ball suspended by a cord from the roof of
the diligence would have given less annoyance to
my unfortunate companions than my poor nodding
head gave as it bobbed on all sides as if it was attached to my neck by a single tendon.   On one side
of me sat a nun, on the other a boy, and opposite a
peasant-woman, and throughout the entire journey I
did nothing but strike my head against these three
victims with the monotonous motion of a bell-clap-
per.   The nun, poor creature! endured the strokes
in silence, perhaps in expiation for her sins of
thought; but the boy and peasant-woman muttered
from time to time, "He is a barbarian!"—"This
must stop!"—"His head is like lead!"   Finally, a
witticism from one of the passengers released all four
of us from this suffering.   The peasant-woman was
lamenting a little louder than usual, and a voice from
the end of the diligence exclaimed, "Be consoled; if
your head is not yet broken, you may be sure it will

not be, for it must certainly be proof against the hammer." They all laughed; I awakened, excused myself, and the three victims were so happy to find themselves released from that cruel thumping that, instead of taking revenge with bitter words, they said, "Poor fellow! you have slept badly. How you must have hurt your head!"

We finally arrived at the railway, and behold what a perverse fate! Although I was alone in the railway-carriage, where I might have slept like a nabob, I could not close my eyes. A pang went through my heart at the thought of having made the journey by night when I could not see anything nor enjoy the distant view of Granada. And I remembered the lovely verses of Martinez de la Rosa:

"O my dear fatherland! At last I see thee again! I see thy fair soil, thy joyful teeming fields, thy glorious sun, thy serene sky!

"Yes! I see the fabled Granada stretching along the plain from hill to hill, her towers rising among her gardens of eternal green, the crystal streams kissing her walls, the noble mountains enclosing her valleys, and the Sierra Nevada crowning the distant horizon.

"Oh, thy memory haunted me wherever I went, Granada! It destroyed my pleasures, my peace, and my glory, and oppressed my heart and soul! By the icy banks of the Seine and the Thames

I remembered with a sigh the happy waters of the Darro and the Genil, and many times, as I carolled a gay ballad, my bitter grief overcame me, and weeping, not to be repressed, choked my voice.

"In vain the delightful Arno displayed her flower-strewn banks, sweet seats of love and peace! 'The plain watered by the gentle Genil.' said I, 'is more flowery, the life of the lovely Granada is more dear.' And I murmured these words as one disconsolate, and, remembering the house of my fathers, I raised my sad eyes to heaven.

"What is thy magic, what thy unspeakable spell, O fatherland! O sweet name! that thou art so dear? The swarthy African, far from his native desert, looks with sad disdain on fields of green; the rude Laplander, stolen from his mother-earth, sighs for perpetual night and snow; and I—I, to whom a kindly fate granted birth and nurture in thy bosom blest by so many gifts of God—though far from thee, could I forget thee, Granada?"

When I reached Granada it was quite dark, and I could not see so much as the outlines of a house. A diligence drawn by two horses,

> " . . . anzi due cavallette
>   Di quella de Mosé lá dell' Egitto,"

landed me at a hotel, where I was kept waiting an hour while my bed was being made, and finally, just

before three o'clock in the morning, I was at last able to lay my head on the pillow. But my troubles were not over: just as I was falling into a doze I heard an indistinct murmur in the next room, and then a masculine voice which said distinctly, " Oh, what a little foot!" You who have bowels of compassion, pity me. The pillow was torn a little; I pulled out two tufts of wool, stuffed them in my ears; and, rehearsing in thought the misfortunes of my journey, I slept the sleep of the just.

In the morning I went out betimes and walked about through the streets of Granada until it was a decent hour to go and drag from his home a young gentleman of Granada whom I had met at Madrid at the house of Fernandez Guerra, Gongora by name, the son of a distinguished archeologist and a descendant of the famous Cordovan poet Luigi Gongora, of whom I spoke in passing. That part of the city which I saw in those few hours did not fulfil my expectation. I had expected to find narrow mysterious streets and white cottages like those of Cordova and Seville, but I found instead spacious squares and some handsome straight streets, and others tortuous and narrow enough, it is true, but flanked by high houses, for the most part painted in false bas-reliefs with cupids and garlands and flourishes and draperies, and hangings of a thousand colors, without the Oriental appearance of the other Andalusian cities.

The lowest part of Granada is almost all laid out
with the regularity of a modern city. As I passed
along those streets I was filled with contempt, and
should certainly have carried a gloomy face to
Señor Gongora if by chance as I walked at random
I had not come out into the famous *Alameda*, which
enjoys the reputation of being the most beautiful
promenade in the world, and it repaid me a thousand times for the detestable regularity of the
streets which lead to it.

Imagine a long avenue of unusual width, along
which fifty carriages might pass abreast, flanked by
other smaller avenues, along which run rows of
measureless trees, which at a noble height form an
immense green arch, so dense that not a sunbeam
can penetrate it, and at the two ends of the central
avenue two monumental fountains throwing up the
water in two great streams which fall again in the
finest vaporous spray, and between the many
avenues crystal streams, and in the middle a garden all roses and myrtle and jessamine and delicate fountains; and on one side the river Genil,
which flows between banks covered with laurel-
groves, and in the distance the snowclad mountains,
upon whose sides distant palms raise their fantastic
fronds; and everywhere a brilliant green, dense
and luxuriant, through which one sees here and
there an enchanting strip of azure sky.

As I turned off of the Alameda I met a great

number of peasants going out of the city, two by two and in groups, with their wives and children, singing and jesting. Their dress did not seem to me different from that of the peasants in the neighborhood of Cordova and Seville. They wore velvet hats, some with very broad brims, others with high brims curved back; a little jacket made with bands of many-colored cloth; a scarf of red or blue; closely-fitting trousers buttoned along the hip; and a pair of leathern gaiters open at the side, so as to show the leg. The women were dressed like those in the other provinces, and even in their faces there was no noticeable difference.

I reached my friend's house and found him buried in his archæological studies, sitting in front of a heap of old medals and historic stones. He received me with delight, with a charming Andalusian courtesy, and, after exchanging the first greetings, we both pronounced with one voice that magic word that in every part of the world stirs a tumult of great recollections in every heart and arouses a sense of secret longing; that gives a final spur toward Spain to one who has the desire to travel thither and has not yet finally resolved to start; that name at which hearts of poets and painters beat faster and the eyes of women flash—"The Alhambra!"

We rushed out of the house.

The 'Alhambra is situated upon a high hill which overlooks the city, and from a distance presents the appearance of a fortress, like almost all Oriental palaces. But when, with Gongora, I climbed the street of *Los Gomeles* on our way toward the famous edifice, I had not yet seen the least trace of a distant wall, and I did not know in what part of the city we should find it. The street of *Los Gomeles* slopes upward and describes a slight curve, so that for a good way one sees only houses ahead, and supposes the Alhambra to be far away. Gongora did not speak, but I read in his face that in his heart he was greatly enjoying the thought of the surprise and delight that I should experience. He looked at the ground with a smile, answering all my questions with a sign which seemed to say, "Wait a minute!" and now and then raised his eyes almost furtively to measure the remaining distance. And I so enjoyed his pleasure that I could have thrown my arms around his neck in gratitude.

We arrived before a great gate that closed the street. "Here we are!" said Gongora. I entered.

I found myself in a great grove of enormously high trees, leaning one toward another, on this side and on that, along a great avenue which climbs the hill and is lost in the shade: so close are the trees that a man could scarcely pass among them, and wherever one looks one sees only their trunks, which close the way like a continuous wall. The branches meet above the avenues; not a sunbeam penetrates the wood; the shade is very dense; on every side glide murmuring streams, and the birds sing, and one feels a vernal freshness in the air.

"We are now in the Alhambra," said Gongora: "turn around, and you will see the towers and the embattled barrier-wall."

"But where is the palace?" I demanded.

"That is a mystery," he answered; "let us go forward at random."

We climbed an avenue running along beside the great central avenue that winds up toward the summit. The trees form overhead a green pavilion through which not a particle of sky is visible, and the grass, the shrubbery, and the flowers make on either side a lovely border, bright and fragrant, sloping slightly toward each other, as if they are trying to unite, mutually attracted by the beauty of their colors and the fragrance of their perfume.

"Let us rest a moment," I said: "I want to take a great breath of this air; it seems to contain some secret germs that if infused into the blood must prolong one's life; it is air redolent of youth and health."

"Behold the door!" exclaimed Gongora.

I turned as if I had been struck in the back, and saw a few steps ahead a great square tower, of a deep-red color, crowned with battlements, with an arched door, above which one sees a key and a hand cut in the stone.

I questioned my guide, and he told me that this was the principal entrance of the Alhambra, and that it was called the Gate of Justice, because the Moorish kings used to pronounce sentence beneath that arch. The key signifies that this door is the key to the fortress, and the hand symbolizes the five cardinal virtues of Islam—Prayer, Fasting, Beneficence, Holy War, and the Pilgrimage to Mecca. The Arabian inscription attests that the edifice was erected four centuries ago by the Sultan Abul Hagag Yusuf, and another inscription, which one sees everywhere on the columns, says, "There is no God but Allah, and Mohammed is his Prophet! and there is no power, no strength, apart from Allah!"

We passed under the arch and continued the ascent along an enclosed street until we found ourselves at the top of the hill, in the middle of an esplanade surrounded by a parapet and dotted with shrubs and flowers. I turned at once toward the valley to enjoy the view, but Gongora seized me by the arm and made me look in the opposite direction. I was standing in front of the great palace of the Renaissance, partly in ruins and flanked by some wretched little houses.

"Is this a joke?" I demanded. "Have you brought me here to see a Moorish castle, for me to find the way closed by a modern palace? Whose abominable idea was it to run up this building in the gardens of the caliphs?"

"Charles V.'s."

"He was a vandal. I have not yet forgiven him for the Gothic church he planted in the middle of the mosque of Cordova, and now these barracks fill me with utter loathing of his crown and his glory. But, in the name of Heaven, where is the Alhambra?"

"There it is."

"Where?"

"Among those huts."

"Oh, fudge!"

"I pledge you my word of honor."

I folded my arms and looked at him, and he laughed.

"Well, then," I exclaimed, "this great name of the Alhambra is only another of those usual false exaggerations of the poets. I, Europe, and the world have been shamefully deceived. Was it worth while to dream of the Alhambra for three hundred and sixty-five nights in succession, and then to come to see a group of ruins with some broken columns and smoky inscriptions?"

"How I enjoy this!" answered Gongora with a peal of laughter. "Cheer up now; come and be persuaded that the world has not been deceived: let us enter this rubbish-pile."

We entered by a little door, crossed a corridor,

and found ourselves in a court. With a sudden cry
I seized Gongora's hand, and he asked with a tone
of triumph,

" Are you persuaded ?"

I did not answer, I did not see him : I was already
far away ; the Alhambra had already begun to exer-
cise upon me that mysterious and powerful fascination which no one can avoid nor any one express.

We were in the *Patio de los Arrayanes*, the Court
of the Myrtles, which is the largest in the edifice,
and presents at once the appearance of a room, a
courtyard, and a garden. A great rectangular basin
full of water, surrounded by a myrtle hedge, extends
from one side of the *patio* to the other, and like a
mirror reflects the arches, arabesques, and the mural
inscriptions.

To the right of the entrance there extend two
orders of Moorish arches, one above the other, supported by slender columns, and on the opposite side
of the court rises a tower with a door through which
one sees the inner rooms in semi-darkness and the
mullioned windows, and through the windows the
blue sky and the summits of the distant mountains.
The walls are ornamented to a certain height from
the pavement with brilliant mosaics, and above the
mosaics with arabesques of very intricate design
that seem to tremble and change at every step, and
here and there among the arabesques and along the
arches they stretch and creep and intertwine, like

garlands, Moorish inscriptions containing greetings, proverbs, and legends.

Beside the door of entrance is written in Cufic characters: Eternal Happiness! — Blessing! — Prosperity!—Felicity!—Praised be God for the blessing of Islam!

In another place it is written: I seek my refuge in the Lord of the Morning.

In another place: O God! to thee belong eternal thanksgiving and undying praise.

Elsewhere there are verses from the Koran and entire poems in praise of the caliphs.

We stood some minutes in silent admiration; not the buzz of a fly was heard; now and then Gongora started toward the tower, but I clutched him by the arm and felt that he was trembling with impatience.

"But we must make haste," said he, finally, "or else we shall not get back to Granada before evening."

"What do I know of Granada?" I answered; "what do I know of morning or evening or of myself? I am in the Orient!"

"But this is only the antechamber of the Alhambra, my dear Arabian," said Gongora, urging me forward. "Come, come with me where it will really seem like being in the Orient."

And he led me, reluctant though I was, to the very threshold of the tower-door. There I turned to look once more at the Court of Myrtles and gave a cry of surprise. Between two slender columns of the arched gallery which faces the tower, on the opposite side of the courtyard, stood a girl, a beautiful dark Andalusian face, with a white mantle wound around her head and falling over her shoulder: she stood leaning upon the railing in a languid attitude, with her eyes fixed upon us. I cannot tell the fantastic effect produced by that figure at that moment—the grace imparted by the arch which curved above the girl's head and the two columns which formed a frame around her, and the beautiful harmony which she gave to the whole court, as if she were an ornament necessary to its architecture conceived in the mind of the architect at the moment he imagined the whole design. She seemed like a sultana awaiting her lord, thinking of another sky and another love. She continued looking at us, and my heart began to beat faster. I questioned my friend with my eyes, as if to be assured that I was not deceived. Suddenly the sultana laughed, dropped her white mantle, and disappeared.

"She is a servant," said Gongora.

Still I remained in the mist.

She was, in fact, a servant of the custodian of the Alhambra who was in the habit of practising that joke upon strangers.

We entered the tower called the Tower of Comares, or, vulgarly, the Tower of the Ambassadors

The interior forms two halls, the first of which is called the Hall of the Barca, and takes its name either from the fact that it is shaped like a boat or because it was called by the Moors the Hall of *Baraka*, or Blessing, a word which might have been contracted by the people into *barca* (a boat.) This hall hardly seems the work of human hands: it is all a vast network of tracery in the form of garlands, rosettes, boughs of trees, and leaves, covering the vaulted ceiling, the arches, and the walls in every part and in every way—closely twining, checkered, climbing higher and higher, and yet marvellously distinct and combined in such a manner that the parts are presented to the eye altogether at a single glance, affording a spectacle of dazzling magnificence and enchanting grace. I approached one of the walls, fixed my eyes upon the extreme point of an arabesque, and tried to follow its windings and turnings: it was impossible; my eye was lost, my mind confused, and all the arabesques from pavement to ceiling seemed to be moving and blending, as if to conceal the thread of their inextricable network. You may make an effort not to look around, to centre your whole attention upon a single spot of the wall, to scan it closely and follow the thread with your finger: it is futile; in a moment the tracery is a tangled skein, a veil steals between you and the wall, and your arm falls. The wall seems woven like a web,

wrought like brocade, netted like lace, and veined
like a leaf; one cannot look at it closely nor fix its
design in one's mind: it would be like trying to
count the ants in an anthill: one must be content
to look at the walls with a wandering glance, then
to rest and look again later, and then to think of
something else and talk. After I had looked around
a little with the air of a man overcome with vertigo
rather than admiration, I turned toward Gongora,
so that he might read in my face what I would have
spoken.

"Let us enter the other pile of ruins," he answered with a smile as he drew me into the great
Hall of the Ambassadors, which fills all the interior
of the tower, for, really, the Hall of the *Barca*
belongs to a little building which does not form a
part of the tower, although it is joined to it. The
tower is square in form, spacious, and lighted with
nine great arched windows in the form of doors,
which present almost the appearance of so many
alcoves, so great is the thickness of the wall; each
one is divided down the middle toward the outside
by a little marble column that supports two beautiful arches surmounted in their turn by two little
arched windows. The walls are covered with
mosaics and arabesques indescribably delicate and
multiform, and with innumerable inscriptions extending like wide embroidered ribbons over the arches
of the windows, up the massive cornices, along the

friezes, and around the niches where once stood vases full of flowers and perfumed water. The ceiling, which rises to a great height, is inlaid with cedar-wood, white, gold, and azure, joined together in circles, stars, and crowns, and forming many little arches, cells, and vaulted windows, through which falls a wavering light, and from the cornice which joins the ceiling to the walls hang tablets of stucco-work cut in facets chiselled and moulded like. stalactites and bunches of flowers. The throne stood at the central window on the side opposite the door of entrance. From the windows on that side one enjoys a stupendous view of the valley of the Darro, deep and silent, as if it too felt the fascination of the Alhambra's grandeur; from the windows on the other two sides one sees the boundary-wall and the towers of the fortress; and through the entrance the light arches of the Court of the Myrtles in the distance and the water of the basin, which reflects the blue of the sky.

"Well!" Gongora demanded; "was it worth dreaming of the Alhambra for three hundred and sixty-five nights?"

"There is a strange thought passing through my brain at this moment," I replied. "That court as it looks from here, that hall, those windows, those colors, everything that surrounds me, seems familiar; it seems to correspond with a picture which I have carried in my head I know not how long and I know not in what manner, confused with a thousand other things, perhaps born of a dream—how should I know? When I was sixteen years old I was a lover, and the young girl and I alone in a garden in the shade of a summer-house, as we gazed in each other's eyes, uttered unconsciously a cry of joy that stirred our blood as if it had come from the mouth of a third person who had discovered our secret. Well, since that time I have often longed to be a king and to have a palace; but in giving form to that desire my imagination did not rest merely in the grand gilded palaces of our country; it flew to distant lands, and there on the summit of a lofty mountain reared a castle of its own in which everything was small and graceful and illumined by a mysterious light; and there were long suites of rooms adorned with a thousand fanciful and delicate ornaments, with windows through which we two alone might look, and little columns behind which my little one might almost hide her face playfully as she listened to my step approaching from hall to hall, or heard my voice mingled with the murmur of the fountains in the garden. All unconsciously, in building that castle in fantasy, I was building the Alhambra; in those moments I imagined some-thing like these halls, these windows, and this court that we see before us—so similar, indeed, that the more I look around the better I remember and seem to recognize the place just as I have seen it a thousand times. All lovers dream a little of the Alhambra, and if they were able to reproduce all their dreams in line and color, they would make pictures that would amaze us by their likeness to all one sees here. This architecture does not express power, glory, and grandeur; it expresses love and passion —love with its mysteries, its caprices, its fervor, its bursts of God-given gratitude; passion with its melancholy and its silences. There is, then, a close connection, a harmony, between the beauty of this Alhambra and the souls of those who have loved at sixteen, when longings are but dreams and visions. And hence arises the indescribable fascination exercised by this beauty, and hence the Alhambra, although deserted and ruined as it is, is still the most enchanting castle in the world, and to the end of time visitors will leave it with a tear. For in parting with the Alhambra we bid a last adieu to the most beautiful dreams of youth revived among these walls for the last time. We bid adieu to faces unspeakably dear that have broken the oblivion of many years to stand beside us a last time by the little columns of these windows. We bid adieu to all the fancies of youth. We bid adieu to that love which will never live again."

"It is true," answered my friend, "but what will you say when you have seen the Court of the Lions? Come, let us hurry."

We left the tower with hasty steps, crossed the

Court of Myrtles, and came to a little door opposite
the door of entrance.

"Stop!" cried Gongora.

I stopped.

"Do me a favor?"

"A hundred."

"Only one: shut your eyes and don't open them
until I tell you."

"Well, they are shut."

"See that you keep them so; I sha'n't like it if
you open them."

"Never fear."

Gongora took me by the hand and led me forward:
I trembled like a leaf.

We took about fifteen steps and stopped.

"Look!" said Gongora in an agitated voice.

I looked, and I swear by the head of my reader I
felt two tears trickling down my cheeks.

We were in the Court of the Lions.

If at that moment I had been obliged to go out as
I had come in, I could not have told what I had seen.
A forest of columns, a vision of arches and tracery,
an indefinable elegance, an unimaginable delicacy,
prodigious wealth; an irrepressible sense of air-
iness, transparency, and wavy motion like a great
pavilion of lace; an appearance as of an edifice
which must dissolve at a breath; a variety of lights
and mysterious shadows; a confusion, a capricious
disorder, of little things; the grandeur of a castle,

the gayety of a summer-house; an harmonious grace,
an extravagance, a delight; the fancy of an enamored girl, the dream of an angel; a madness, a
nameless something,—such is the first effect of the
Court of the Lions.

The court is not larger than a great ball-room; it
is rectangular in form, with walls no higher than a
two-storied Andalusian cottage. A light portico
runs all around, supported by very slender white
marble columns grouped in symmetrical disorder, two
by two and three by three, almost without pedestals, so
that they are like the trunks of trees standing on the
ground: they have varied capitals, high and graceful, in the form of little pilasters, above which bend
little arches of very graceful form, which do not
seem to rest upon the columns, but rather to be
suspended over them like curtains upholding the
columns themselves and resembling ribbons and
twining garlands. From the middle of the two
shortest sides advance two groups of columns forming two little square temples of nine arches in the
form of stalactites, fringes, pendants, and tassels that
seem as though they ought to swing and become
tangled with the slightest breeze. Large Arabian
inscriptions run along the four walls, over the arches,
around the capitals, and along the walls of the little
temple. In the middle of the court rises a great
marble basin supported by twelve lions and surrounded by a paved channel, from which flow four

other smaller channels that make a cross between
the four sides of the court, cross the portico, enter
the adjoining rooms, and join the other water-courses
which surround the entire edifice. Behind the two
two little temples and in the middle of the other two
sides there appear halls and suites of rooms with
great open doors, through which one can see the
dark background broken by the white columns,
gleaming as if they stood at the mouth of a grotto.
At every step the forest of columns seems to move
and rearrange itself in a new way; behind a
column that is apparently single spring up two,
three, a row of columns; some fade away, others
unite, and still others separate: on looking back
from the end of one of the halls everything appears
different; the arches on the opposite side seem very
far away; the columns appear out of place; the little temples have changed their form; one sees new
arches rising beyond the walls, and new columns
gleaming here in the sunlight, there in the shadow,
yonder scarcely visible by the dim light which sifts
through the tracery of the stucco, and the farthest
lost in the darkness. There is a constant variety of
scene, distance, deceptive effects, mysteries, and
playful tricks of the eye, produced by the architecture, the sun, and one's heightened imagination.

" What must this *patio* have been," said Gongora,
" when the inner walls of the portico were resplend-
ent with mosaics, the capitals of the columns flashed

with gold, the ceilings and vaults were painted in
a thousand colors, the doors hung with silken curtains, the niches full of flowers, and under the little
temples and through the halls ran streams of perfumed water, and from the nostrils of the lions
spurted twelve jets which fell into the basin, and
the air was heavy with the most delicious perfumes
of Arabia!"

We remained in the court over an hour, and the
time passed like a flash; and I too did what all have
done in that place—Spaniards and foreigners alike,
men and women, poets and those who are not poets.
I ran my hand along the walls, touched all the little
columns, clasped them one by one with my two hands
like the waist of a child, hid among them, counted
them, looked at them from a hundred directions,
crossed the court in a hundred ways; tried if it were
true that by speaking a word in a deep voice in the
mouth of one of the lions you could hear it distinctly from the mouths of all the others; searched
along the marbles for the blood-spots of the romantic
legends, and wearied my eyes and brain in following
the arabesques. There were a number of ladies
present. In the Court of the Lions ladies show every
sort of childish delight: they look out between two
twin columns, hide in the dark corners, sit on the
floor, and stand for hours motionless, resting their
heads upon their hands, dreaming. These ladies did
likewise. There was one dressed in white who, as

she passed behind the distant columns, when she
thought no one saw her assumed a certain majestic
air, like a melancholy sultana, and then laughed
with one of her friends : it was enchanting.

"Let us go," said my friend.

"Let us go," I replied, and could not move a step.
I was experiencing not only a delightful sense of
surprise, but I was trembling with pleasure, and was
filled with a longing to touch, to probe, and in some
way to see behind those walls and those columns, as
if they were made of some secret material and ought
to disclose in their inmost part the first cause of the
fascination which the place exerts. In all my life I
have never thought or said, or shall ever say, so
many fond words, so many foolish expressions, so
many pretty, happy, senseless things, as I thought
and said at that hour.

"But one must come here at sunrise," said Gongora, "one must come at sunset, or at night when
the moon is full, to see the miracles of color, light,
and shade. It is enough to make one lose one's
head."

We went to see the halls. On the eastern side is
the Hall of Justice, which is reached by passing
under three great arches, each of which corresponds
with a door opening into the court. It is a long, narrow hall, with intricate arabesques and precious mosaics, and its vaulted ceiling all points and hollows
and clusters of stucco that hang down from the

arches and run along the walls, clustered together here and there, drooping, growing one out of the other, crowding and overtopping each other, so that they seem to dispute the space like the bubbles in boiling water, and still presenting in many parts traces of old colors that must have given the ceiling the appearance of a pavilion covered with flowers and hanging fruit. The hall has three little alcoves, in each of which one may see a Moorish painting, to which time and the extreme rarity of works remaining from the brush of Moorish artists have given a very high value. The paintings are on leather, and the leather is fastened to the wall. In the central alcove there are painted on a golden ground ten men, supposed to be ten kings of Granada, clothed in white, with cowls on their heads and scimetars in their hands, sitting on embroidered cushions. The paintings in the other two alcoves represent castles, ladies and cavaliers, hunting scenes, and love episodes whose significance it is difficult to understand. But the faces of the ten kings are marvellously true to the picture one has formed of their race: there is the dark olive complexion, the sensuous lips, the black eyes, with an intense mysterious glance that seems always to be shining in the dark corners of the halls of the Alhàmbra.

On the north side of the court there is another hall, called the hall *De las dos Hermanas* (of the two sisters), so called from two great marble slabs which

form the pavement. It is the most beautiful hall in
the Alhambra—a little square arched room, with one
of those ceilings in the form of a cupola which the
Spaniards call half oranges, supported by slender
columns and arches arranged in a circle, all adorned,
like a grotto full of stalactites, with an infinite number of points and hollows, colored and gilded, and
so light to the view that it seems as if they are
suspended in the air, and would tremble at a touch
like a curtain or separate like a cloud or disappear
like a cluster of soap-bubbles. The walls, like those
of all the other halls, are bedecked with stucco and
carved with arabesques incredibly intricate and delicate, forming one of the most marvellous works of
human patience and imagination. The more one
looks, the more numberless become the lines which
blend and cross, and from one figure springs another,
and from that a third, and all three produce a fourth
that has escaped the eye, and this divides suddenly
into ten other figures that have passed unnoticed,
and then they mingle again and are again transformed; and one never ceases to discover new combinations, for when the first reappear they are
already forgotten, and produce the same effect as at
the beginning. One would lose sight and reason in
trying to comprehend that labyrinth: it would require an hour to study the outlines of a window, the
ornaments of a pilaster, and the arabesques of a
frieze; an hour would not be sufficient to fix upon

the mind the design of one of the stupendous cedar
doors. On either side of the hall there are two
little alcoves, and in the centre a little basin with a
pipe for a fountain that empties into the channel that
crosses the portico and flows to the Fountain of the
Lions.

Directly opposite the entrance there is another
door, through which one passes into another long,
narrow room called the Hall of the Oranges. And
from this hall, through a third door, one enters a
little chamber called the Cabinet of Lindaraja, very
richly ornamented, at the end of which there is a
graceful window with two arches overlooking a
garden.

To enjoy all the beauty of this magical architecture one must leave the Hall of the Two Sisters,
cross the Court of the Lions, and enter a room called
the Hall of the Abencerrages, which lies on the
southern side, opposite the Hall of the Two Sisters, to
which it is very similar in form and ornamentation.
From the end of this hall one looks across the
Court of the Lions through the Hall of the Two
Sisters into the Hall of the Oranges and even into
the Cabinet of Lindaraja and the garden beyond,
where a mass of verdure appears under the arches
of that jewel of a window. The two sides of this
window, so diminutive and full of light when seen in
the distance from the end of that suite of darkened
rooms, look like two great open eyes, that look at

you and make you imagine that beyond them must lie the unfathomable mysteries of paradise.

After seeing the Hall of the Abencerrages we went to see the baths, which are situated between the Hall of the Two Sisters and the Court of the Myrtles. We descended a flight of stairs, passed a long narrow corridor, and came out into a splendid hall called the hall *De las Divans*, where the favorites of the king came to rest on their Persian rugs to the sound of the lyre after they had bathed in the adjoining rooms. This hall was reconstructed on the plans of the ancient ruins, and adorned with arabesques, gilded and painted, by Spanish artists after the ancient patterns; consequently one may consider it a room of the Moorish period remaining intact in every part. In the middle is a fountain, and in the opposite walls are two alcoves where the women reposed on divans, and overhead the galleries where the musicians played. The walls are laced, dotted, checkered, and mottled with a thonsand brilliant hues, presenting the appearance of a tapestry of Chinese stuff shot with golden threads, with an endless interweaving of figures that must have maddened the most patient mosaic-worker on earth.

Nevertheless, a painter was at work in the hall. He was a German who had worked for three months in copying the walls. Gongora knew him, and asked, "It is wearisome work, is it not?"

And he answered with a smile, "I don't find it so," and bent again over his picture.

I looked at him as if he had been a creature from another world.

We entered the little bathing-chambers, vaulted and lighted from above by some star- and flower-shaped apertures in the wall. The bathing-tubs are very large, single blocks of marble enclosed between two walls. The corridors which lead from one room to the other are low and narrow, so that a man can scarcely pass through them; they are delightfully cool. As I stood looking into one of these little rooms I was suddenly impressed with a sad thought.

"What makes you sad?" asked my friend.

"I was thinking," I replied, "of how we live, summer and winter, in houses like barracks, in rooms on the third floor, which are either dark or else flooded with a torrent of light, without marble, without water, without flowers, without columns; I was thinking that we must live so all our lives and die between those walls without once experiencing the delights of these charmed palaces; I was thinking that even in this wretched earthly life one may enjoy vastly, and that I shall not share this enjoyment at all; I was thinking that I might have been born four centuries ago a king of Granada, and that I was born instead a poor man."

My friend laughed, and, taking my arm between

his thumb and finger, as if to give me a pinch, he said, " Don't think of that. Think of how much beauty, grace, and mystery these tubs must have seen; of the little feet that have played in their perfumed waters; of the long hair which has fallen over their rims; of the great languid eyes that have looked at the sky through the openings in the vaulted ceiling, while beneath the arches of the Court of the Lions sounded the hastening step of an impatient caliph, and the hundred fountains of the castle sighed with a quickening murmur, ' Come! come! come!' and in a perfumed hall a trembling slave reverently closed the windows with the rose-colored curtains."

" Ah! leave my soul in peace!" I replied, shrugging my shoulders.

We crossed the garden of the Cabinet of Lindaraja and a mysterious court called the *Patio de la Reja*, and by a long gallery that commands a view of the country reached the top of one of the farthest towers of the Alhambra, called the *Mirador de la Reina* (the Queen's toilet), shaded by a little pavilion and open all round, hanging over an abyss like an eagle's nest. The view one enjoys from this point—one may say it without fear of contradiction—has not its equal on the face of the earth.

Imagine an immense plain, green as a meadow, covered with young grass, crossed in all directions

by endless rows of cypresses, pines, oaks, and
poplars, dotted with dense orange-groves that in the
distance look no larger than shrubs, and with great
orchards and gardens so crowded with fruit trees
that they look like green hillocks; and the river
Xenil winding through this immense plain, gleaming
among the groves and gardens like a great silver
ribbon; and all around wooded hills, and beyond
the hills lofty rocks of fantastic form, which complete the picture of a barrier-wall with gigantic
towers separating that earthly paradise from the
world; and there, just beneath one's eyes, the city
of Granada, partly extending to the plain and partly
on the slope of the hill, all interspersed with groups
of trees, shapeless masses of verdure which rise and
wave above the roofs of the houses like enormous
plumes, until it seems as if they were striving to ex-
pand and unite and cover the entire city; and still
nearer the deep valley of the Darro more than
covered—yes, filled to overflowing and almost
heaped full—with its prodigious growth of vegetation, rising like a mountain, and above it there rises
yet again a grove of gigantic poplars tossing their
topmost boughs so close under the windows of the
tower that one can almost touch them; and to the
right beyond the Darro, on a high hill towering
toward heaven, bold and rounded like a cupola, the
palace of the Generalife, encircled by its aërial
gardens and almost hidden in a grove of laurels,

poplars, and pomegranates; and in the opposite
direction a marvellous spectacle, a thing incredible,
a vision of a dream—the Sierra Nevada, after the
Alps, the highest mountain-range in Europe crowned
with snow, white even to a few miles from the gates
of Granada, white even to the hills on whose sides
spread the pomegranates and palms, and where a
vegetation almost tropical expands in all its splendid
pomp.

Imagine now over this vast paradise, containing
all the smiling graces of the Orient and all the severe beauties of the North, wedding Europe to
Africa, and bringing to the nuptials all the choicest
marvels of nature, and exhaling to heaven all the
perfumes of the earth blended in one breath,—imagine above this happy valley the sky and sun of
Andalusia, rolling on to its setting and tinting the
peaks with a divine rose-color, and painting the
mountain-sides of the Sierra with all the colors of
the rainbow, and clothing them with all the reflections of the most limpid azure pearls, its rays breaking in a thousand mists of gold, purple, and gray
upon the rocks encircling the plain, and, as it sinks
in a flame of fire, casting like a last good-night a
luminous crown about the gloomy towers of the Alhambra and the flower-crowned pinnacles of the
Generalife, and tell me if this world can give anything more solemn, more glorious, more intoxicating
than this love-feast of the earth and sky, before

which for nine centuries Granada has trembled with delight and throbbed with pride?

The roof of the *Mirador de la Reina* is supported by little Moorish columns, between which extend flattened arches which give the pavilion an extremely fanciful and graceful appearance. The walls are frescoed, and one may see along the friezes the initials of Isabella and Philip interwoven with cupids and flowers. Close by the door there still remains a stone of the ancient pavement, all perforated, upon which it is said the sultanas sat to be enveloped in the clouds of perfumed vapor which arose from below.

Everything in this place tells of love and happiness. There one breathes an air as pure as that on a mountain-peak, there one perceives a mingled fragrance of myrtles and roses, and no other sound reaches the ear save the murmur of the Darro as it dashes among the rocks of its stony bed, and the singing of a thousand birds hidden in the dense foliage of the valley; it is truly a nest of loves, a hanging alcove where to go and dream of an aërial balcony to which one might climb and thank God for being happy.

" Ah, Gongora," I exclaimed after contemplating for some moments that enchanting spectacle, " I would give years of my life to be able to summon here, with a stroke of a magic wand, all the dear ones who are looking for me in Italy."

Gongora pointed out a large space on the wall, all black with dates and names of visitors to the Alhambra, written with crayon and charcoal and cut with knives.

" What is this written here ?" he demanded.

I approached and uttered a cry: " Chateaubriand !"

" And here ?"

" Byron !"

" And here ?"

" Victor Hugo !"

After descending from the *Mirador de la Reina* I thought I had seen the Alhambra, and was so imprudent as to tell my friend so. If he had had a stick in his hand, I verily believe he would have struck me ; but, as he had not, he contented himself by regarding me with the air of one demanding whether or not I had lost my senses.

We returned to the Court of the Myrtles and visited the rooms situated on the other side of the Tower of Comares, the greater part in ruins, the rest altered, some absolutely bare, without either pavement or roof, but all worth seeing, both in remembrance of what they had been and for the sake of understanding the plan of the edifice. The ancient mosque was converted into a chapel by Charles V., and a great Moorish hall was changed into an oratory; here and there one still sees the fragments of arabesques and carved ceilings of cedar-wood; the galleries, the courts, and the vestibules remind one of a palace dismantled by fire.

After seeing that part of the Alhambra I really thought there was nothing else left to see, and a second time was imprudent enough to say so to Gongora: this time he could no longer contain himself, and, leading me into a vestibule of the Court of Myrtles and pointing to a map of the building hanging on the wall, he said, " Look, and you will see that all the rooms of the courts and the towers that we have so far visited do not occupy one-twentieth part of the space embraced within the walls of the Alhambra; you will see that we have not yet visited the remains of the three other mosques, the ruins of the House of Cadi, the water-tower, the tower of the Infantas, the tower of the Prisoner, the tower of Candil, the tower of the Picos, the tower of the Daggers, the tower of the *Siete Suelos*, the tower of the Captain, the tower of the Witch, the tower of the Heads, the tower of Arms, the tower of the Hidalgos, the tower of the Cocks, the tower of the Cube, the tower of Homage, the tower of Vela, the Powder Tower, the remains of the House of Mondejar, the military quarters, the iron gate, the inner walls, the cisterns, the promenades; for I would have you know that the Alhambra is not a palace: it is a city, and one could spend his life in studying its arabesques, reading its inscriptions, and every day discovering a new view of the hills and mountains, and going

into ecstasies regularly once every twenty-four
hours."

And I thought I had seen the Alhambra!

On that day I did not wish to learn anything
more, and the dear knows how my head ached when
I returned to the hotel. The day after, at the peep
of dawn, I was back at the Alhambra, and again in
the evening, and I continued to go there every day
so long as I remained at Granada, with Gongora,
with other friends, with guides, or alone; and the Alhambra always seemed vaster and more beautiful
as I wandered through the courts and halls, and
passed hour after hour sitting among the columns or
gazing out of the windows with an ever-heightening
pleasure, every time discovering new beauties, and
ever abandoning myself to those vague and delightful fancies among which my mind had strayed on the
first day. I cannot tell through which entrances my
friends led me into the Alhambra, but I remember
that every day on going there I saw walls and towers
and deserted streets that I had not seen before, and
the Alhambra seemed to me to have changed its site,
to have been transformed, and surrounded as if by
enchantment with new buildings that changed its
original appearance. Who could describe the beauty
of those sunset views; those fantastic groves flooded
with moonlight; the immense plain and the snow-
covered mountains on clear, serene nights; the imposing outlines of those enormous walls, superb

towers, and those measureless trees under a starry sky; the prolonged rustling of those vast masses of verdure overflowing the valleys and climbing the hillsides? It was a spectacle before which my companions remained speechless, although they were born in Granada and accustomed from infancy to look upon these scenes. So we would walk along in silence, each buried in his own thoughts, with hearts oppressed by mild melancholy, and sometimes our eyes were wet with tears, and we raised our faces to heaven with a burst of gratitude and love.

On the day of my arrival at Granada, when I entered the hotel at midnight, instead of finding silence and quiet, I found the *patio* illuminated like a ball-room, people sipping sherbet at the tables, coming and going along the galleries, laughing and talking, and I was obliged to wait an hour before going to sleep. But I passed that hour very pleasantly. While I stood looking at a map of Spain on the wall a great burly fellow, with a face as red as a beet and a great stomach extending nearly to his knees, approached me and, touching his cap, asked if I was an Italian. I replied that I was, and he continued with a smile, "And so am I; I am the proprietor of the hotel."

"I am delighted to hear it, the more so because I see you are making money."

"Great Heavens!" he replied in a tone which he wished to seem melancholy. "Yes, . . . I cannot

complain; but, . . . believe me, my dear sir, however well things may go, when one is far from his
native land one always feels a void here;" and he
put his hand upon his enormous chest.

I looked at his stomach.

"A great void," repeated mine host; "one never
forgets one's country. . . . From what province are
you, sir?"

"From Liguria.   And you?"

"From Piedmont. Liguria! Piedmont! Lombardy!
They are countries!"

"They are fine countries, there is no doubt of
that, but, after all, you cannot complain of Spain.
You are living in one of the most beautiful cities in
the world, and are proprietor of one of the finest
hotels in the city; you have a crowd of guests all
the year round, and then I see you enjoy enviable
health."

"But the void?"

I looked again at his stomach.

"Oh, I see, sir; but you are deceived, you know,
if you judge me by appearances.   You cannot imagine what a pleasure it is when an Italian comes here.
What you will?   Weakness it may be. . . . I know
not, . . . but I should like to see him every day at
table, and I believe that if my wife did not laugh at
me I should send him a dozen dishes on my own
account, as a foretaste."

"At what hour do you dine to-morrow?"

"At five. But, after all, . . . one eats little here, . . . hot country, . . . everybody lives lightly, . . . whatever their nationality may be. . . . That is the rule. . . . But you have not seen the other Italian who is here?"

So saying, he turned around, and a man came forward from a corner of the court where he had been watching us. The proprietor, after a few words, left us alone. The stranger was a man of about forty, miserably dressed, who spoke through closed teeth, and kept continually clenching his hands with a convulsive motion as if he was making an effort to keep from using his fists. He told me he was a chorus-singer from Lombardy, and that he had arrived the day before at Granada with other artists booked to sing at the opera for the summer season.

"A beastly country!" he exclaimed without any preamble, looking around as if he wished to make a speech.

"Then you do not remain in Spain voluntarily?" I asked.

"In Spain? I? Excuse me: it is just as if you had asked me whether I was staying voluntarily in a galley."

"But why?"

"Why? But can't you see what sort of people the Spaniards are—ignorant, superstitious, proud, blood-thirsty, impostors, thieves, charlatans, villains?"

And he stood a moment motionless in a questioning attitude, with the veins of his neck so swollen that they seemed ready to burst.

"Pardon me," I replied; "your judgment does not seem favorable enough to admit of my agreeing with you. When it comes to ignorance, excuse me, it will not do for us Italians, for us who still have cities where the schoolmasters are stoned and the professors are stabbed if they give a zero to their scholars,—it will not do for us, I say, to pick flaws in others. As for superstition, alas for us again! since we may still see in that city of Italy in which popular instruction is most widely diffused an unspeakable uproar over a miraculous image of the Madonna found by a poor ignorant woman in the middle of a street! As for crime, I frankly declare that if I were obliged to draw a comparison between the two countries before an audience of Spaniards, with the statistics now in hand, without first proving my data and conclusions, I should be very much alarmed. . . . I do not wish to say by this that we are not, on the whole, sailing in smoother water than is Spain. I wish to say that an Italian in judging the Spanish, if he would be just, must be indulgent."

"Excuse me: I don't think so. A country without political direction! a country a prey to anarchy! a country— Come, now, cite me one great Spaniard of the present day."

"I cannot, . . . there are so few great men any-where."

"Cite me a Galileo."

"Oh, there are no Galileos."

"Cite me a Ratazzi."

"Well, they have none."

"Cite me . . . But, really, they have nothing. And then, does the country seem beautiful to you?"

"Ah! excuse me; that point I will not yield: Andalusia, to cite a single province, is a paradise; Seville, Cadiz, and Granada are splendid cities."

"How? Do you like the houses of Seville and Cadiz, with walls that whiten a poor devil from head to foot whenever he happens to touch them? Do you like those streets along which one can hardly pass after a good dinner? And do you find the An-dalusian women beautiful with their devilish eyes? Come, now, you are too indulgent. They are not a *serious* people. They have summoned Don Amadeus, and now they don't want him. They are not worthy of being governed by a *civilized man*." (These were his actual words.)

"Then you don't find any good in Spain?"

"Not the least."

"But why do you stay?"

"I stay . . . because I make my living here."

"Well, that is something."

"But what a living! It is a dog's life! Every-body knows what Spanish cooking is."

"Excuse me: instead of living like a dog in Spain, why not go and live like a man in Italy?"

Here the poor artist seemed somewhat disconcerted, and I, to relieve his annoyance, offered him a cigar, which he took and lighted without a word. And he was not the only Italian in Spain who had spoken to me in those terms of the country and its inhabitants, denying even the clearness of the sky and the grace of the Andalusian women. I do not know what enjoyment there can be in travelling after this fashion, with the heart closed to every kindly sentiment, and continually on the lookout to censure and despise, as if everything good and beautiful which one finds in a foreign country has been stolen from our own, and as if we are of no account unless we run down everybody else. The people who travel in such a mental attitude make me pity rather than condemn them, because they voluntarily deprive themselves of many pleasures and comforts. So it appears to me, at least, to judge others by myself, for wherever I go the first sentiment which the sights and the people inspire in me is a feeling of sympathy; a desire not to find anything which I shall be obliged to censure; an inclination to imagine every beautiful thing more beautiful; to conceal the unpleasant things, to excuse the defects, to be able to say candidly to myself and others that I am content with everything and everybody. And to arrive at this end I do not have to make

any effort: everything presents itself almost spon-
taneously in its most pleasing aspect, and my imagination benignly paints the other aspects a delicate
rose-color. I know well that one cannot study a
country in this way, nor write sage essays, nor
acquire fame as a profound thinker; but I know
that one travels with a peaceful mind, and that such
travels are of unspeakable benefit.

The next day I went to see the Generalife, which
was a sort of villa of the Moorish kings, and whose
name is linked to that of the Alhambra as is that
of the Alhambra to Granada; but now only a few
arches and arabesques remain of the ancient Generalife. It is a small palace, simple and white, with
few windows, and an arched gallery surrounded with
a terrace, and half hidden in the midst of a grove
of laurel and myrtles, standing on the summit of a
mountain covered with flowers, rising upon the right
bank of the Darro opposite the hill of the Alhambra.
In front of the façade of the palace extends a little
garden, and other gardens rise one above another
almost in the form of a vast staircase to the very
top of the mountain, where there extends a very
high terrace that encloses the Generalife. The
avenues of the gardens and the wide staircases that
lead from one to another of the flower-beds are
flanked by high espaliers' surmounted by arches and
divided by arbors of myrtle, curved and intertwined
with graceful designs, and at every landing-place

rise white summer-houses shaded by trellises and
picturesque groups of orange trees and cypresses.
Water is still as abundant as in Moorish times,
and gives the place a grace, freshness, and luxuriance impossible to describe. From every part
one hears the murmur of rivulets and fountains;
one turns down an avenue and finds a jet of water;
one approaches a window and sees a stream
reaching almost to the window-sill; one enters
a group of trees and the spray of a little water-
fall strikes one's face; one turns and sees water
leaping, running, and trickling through the grass
and shrubbery.

From the height of the terrace one commands
a view of all those gardens as they slope downward
in platforms and terraces; one peers down into
the abyss of vegetation which separates the two
mountains; one overlooks the whole enclosure of
the Alhambra, with the cupolas of its little temples,
its distant towers, and the paths winding among its
ruins; the view extends over the city of Granada
with its plain and its hills, and runs with a single
glance along all the summits of the Sierra Nevada,
that appear so near that one imagines they are not
an hour's walk distant. And while you contemplate
that spectacle your ear is soothed by the murmur
of a hundred fountains and the faint sound of the
bells of the city, which comes in waves scarcely
audible, bearing with it the mysterious fragrance of

this earthly paradise which makes you tremble and grow pale with delight.

Beyond the Generalife, on the summit of a higher mountain, now bleak and bare, there rose in Moorish times other royal palaces, with gardens connected with each other by great avenues lined with myrtle hedges. Now all these marvels of architecture encircled by groves, fountains, and flowers, those fabulous castles in the air, those magnificent and fragrant nests of love and delight, have disappeared, and scarcely a heap of rubbish or a short stretch of wall remains to tell their story to the passer-by. But these ruins, that elsewhere would arouse a feeling of melancholy, do not have such an influence in the presence of that glorious nature whose enchantment not even the most marvellous works of man have ever been able to equal.

On re-entering the city I stopped at one end of the *Carrera del Darro*, in front of a house richly adorned with bas-reliefs representing heraldic shields, armor, cherubs, and lions, with a little balcony, over one corner of which, partly on one wall and partly on another, I read the following mysterious inscription stamped in great letters:

"Esperando la del Cielo,"

which, literally translated, signifies "*Awaiting her in Heaven.*" Curious to learn the hidden meaning of those words, I made a note of them, so that I might

ask the learned father of my friend about them. He
gave me two interpretations, the one almost certainly correct, but not at all romantic; the other romantic, but very doubtful. I give the last: The house
belonged to Don Fernando de Zafra, the secretary of
the Catholic kings. He had a very beautiful daughter.
A young hidalgo, of a family hostile or inferior in
rank to the house of Zafra, became enamored of the
daughter, and, as his love was returned, he asked for
her hand in marriage, but was refused. The refusal
of her father stirred the love of the two young hearts
to flame: the windows of the house were low; the
lover one night succeeded in making the ascent and
entered the maiden's room. Whether he upset a
chair on entering, or coughed, or uttered a low cry
of joy on seeing his beautiful love welcoming him
with open arms, the tradition does not tell, and no
one knows; but certain it is that Don Fernando de
Zafra heard a noise, ran in, saw, and, blind with
fury, rushed upon the ill-fated young man to put
him to death. But he succeeded in making his escape, and Don Fernando in following him ran into
one of his own pages, a partisan of the lovers, who
had helped the hidalgo to enter the house: in his
haste his master mistook him for the betrayer, and,
without hearing his protests and prayers, he had him
bound and hanged from the balcony. The tradition
runs that while the poor victim kept crying, " Pity !
pity !" the outraged father responded as he pointed

toward the balcony, "Thou shalt stay there *esperando la del Cielo!*" (awaiting her in heaven)—a reply which he afterward had cut in the stone walls as a perpetual warning to evil-doers.

I devoted the rest of the day to the churches and monasteries.

The cathedral of Granada deserves to be described part by part in an even higher degree than the cathedral of Malaga, although it too is beautiful and magnificent; but I have already described enough churches. Its foundation was laid by the Catholic kings in 1529 upon the ruins of the principal mosque of the city, but it has never been finished. It has a great façade with three doorways, adorned with statues and bas-reliefs, and it consists of five naves, divided by twenty measureless pilasters, each composed of a bundle of slender columns. The chapels contain paintings by Boccanegra, sculptures by Torrigiano, and tombs and other precious ornaments. Admirable above all is the great chapel, supported by twenty Corinthian columns divided into two orders, upon the first of which rise colossal statues of the twelve apostles, and on the second an entablature covered with garlands and heads of cherubs. Overhead runs a circle of magnificent stained-glass windows, which represent the Passion, and from the frieze which crowns them leap ten bold arches forming the vault of the chapel. Within the arches that support the columns are six great paintings by

Alonzo Cano, which are said to be his most beautiful
and finished work.

And since I have spoken of Alonzo Cano, a native
of Granada, one of the strongest Spanish painters of
the seventeenth century, although a disciple of the
Sevillian school rather than the founder, as some
assert, of a school of his own, but less original than
his greatest contemporaries,—since I have spoken of
him, I wish here to record some traits of his genius
and anecdotes of his life little known outside of Spain,
although exceedingly remarkable. Alonzo Cano was
the most quarrelsome, the most irascible, and the
most violent of the Spanish painters. He spent his
life in contention. He was a priest. From 1652 to
1658, for six consecutive years, without a day's in-
termission, he wrangled with the canons of the cathedral of Granada, of which he was steward, because
he was not willing to become subdeacon in accordance with the stipulated agreement; before leaving
Granada he broke into pieces with his own hands a
statue of Saint Anthony of Padua which he had
made to the order of an auditor of the chancery,
because the man allowed himself to observe that the
price demanded seemed a little dear. Chosen master of design to the royal prince, who, as it appears,
was not born with a talent for painting, he so exas-
perated his pupil that the boy was obliged to have
recourse to the king that he might be taken out of
his hands. Remanded to Granada, to the neighbor-

hood of the chapter of the cathedral, as an especial favor, he bore such a deep rancor from his old litigations with his canons that throughout his life he would not do a stroke of work for them. But this is a small matter. He nursed a blind, bestial, inextinguishable hatred against the Hebrews, and was firmly convinced that in any way to touch a Hebrew or any object that a Hebrew had touched would bring him misfortune. Owing to this conviction he did some of the most extravagant feats in the world. If in walking along the street he ran against a Jew, he would strip off the infected garment and return home in his shirt-sleeves. If by chance he succeeded in discovering that in his absence a servant had admitted a Jew into the house, he discharged the servant, threw away the shoes with which he had touched the pavement profaned by the circumcised, and sometimes even had the pavement torn up and reset. And he found something to find fault with even as he was dying. When he was approaching the end of life the confessor handed him a clumsily-made crucifix that he might kiss it, but he pushed it away with his hand, saying, "Father, give me a naked cross, that I may worship Jesus Christ as He Himself is and as I behold Him in my mind." But, after all, his was a rare, charitable nature which abhorred every vulgar action, and loved with a deep and very pure love the art in which he remains immortal.

On returning to the church after I had made the
round of all the chapels and was preparing to leave,
I was impressed by a suspicion that there was something else still to be seen. I had not read the Guide-
book and had been told nothing, but I heard an
inner voice which said to me, " Seek !" and, in fact,
I sought with my eyes in every direction, without
knowing what I sought. A cicerone noticed me and
sidled up to me, as all of his kind do, like an assassin, and asked me with an air of mystery, " *Quiere
usted algo ?*" (Do you wish something, sir ?)

" I should like to know," I replied, " if there is
anything to see in this cathedral besides that which
I have seen already ?"

" How !" exclaimed the cicerone ; " you have not
seen the royal chapel, have you, sir ?"

" What is there in the royal chapel ?"

" What is there ? Caramba ! Nothing less than
the tombs of Ferdinand and Isabella the Catholics."

I could have said so ! I had in my mind a place
ready for this idea, and the idea was lacking ! The
Catholic kings must certainly have been buried in
Granada, where they fought the last great chivalrous
war of the Middle Ages, and where they gave Christopher Columbus a commission to fit out ships which
bore him to the New World. I ran rather than
walked to the royal chapel, preceded by the limping
cicerone ; an old sacristan opened the door of the
sacristy, and before he allowed me to enter and see

the tombs he led me to a sort of glass cupboard full of precious objects, and said to me, " You will remember that Isabella the Catholic, to furnish Christopher Columbus with the money that he needed to supply the ships for the voyage, not knowing where to turn because the coffers of the state were empty, put her jewels in pawn."

" Yes: well?" I demanded impatiently; and, divining the answer, felt my heart beat faster the while.

" Well," replied the sacristan, " that is the box in which the queen locked her jewels to send them to be pawned."

And so saying he opened the cupboard and took out the box and handed it to me.

Oh! brave men may say what they will; as for me, there are things that make me tremble and weep. I have touched the box that contained the treasure by which Columbus was enabled to discover América. Every time I repeat those words my blood is stirred, and I add, " I have touched it with these hands," and I look at my hands.

· That cupboard contains also the sword of King Ferdinand, the crown and sceptre of Isabella, a missal and some other ornaments of the king and queen.

We entered the chapel. Between the altar and a great iron chancel that separates it from the remaining space stand two great mausoleums of marble adorned with statuettes and bas-reliefs of great value.   Upon one of them lie the statues of Ferdinand and Isabella in their royal robes, with crown, sword, and sceptre ; on the other the statues of the other two princes of Spain, and around the statues lions, angels, and arms, and various ornaments, presenting a regal appearance, austere and magnificent.

The sacristan lighted a flambeau, and, pointing out a sort of trap-door in the pavement between the two mausoleums, asked me to open it and descend into the subterranean chamber.   With the cicerone's aid I opened the trap-door ; the sacristan descended, and I followed him down a narrow little staircase until we reached a little room.   There were five caskets of lead, bound with iron bands, each sealed with two initials under a crown.   The sacristan lowered the torch, and, touching all five of them, one after another, with his hand, said in a slow, solemn voice,

" Here rests the great queen Isabella the Catholic.

" Here rests the great king Ferdinand V.

" Here rests the king Philip I.

" Here rests Queen Joanna the Mad.

" Here rests Lady Maria, her daughter, who died at the age of nine years.

" God keep them all in his holy peace !"

And, placing the torch on the ground, he crossed his arms and closed his eyes, as if to give me time for meditation.

One would become a hunchback at his desk if he

were to describe all the religious monuments of Granada—the stupendous Cartuja ; the Monte Sacro, containing the grottoes of the martyrs ; the church of San Geronimo, where the great leader Gonzalez di Cordova is buried ; the convent of Santo Domingo, founded by Torquemada the Inquisitor ; the convent of the Angels, containing paintings by Cano and Murillo and many others ; but I suppose that my readers may be even more weary than I am, and will consequently pardon me for passing by a mountain of description which probably would only give them a confused idea of the things described.

But as I have mentioned the sepulchre of the great commander, Gonzalez di Cordova, I cannot forbear translating a curious document in reference to him which was shown me in the church of San Geronimo by a sacristan who was an admirer of the deeds of that hero. The document, in the form of an anecdote, is as follows :

"Every step of the great captain Don Gonzalez di Cordova was an assault, and every assault a victory ; his sepulchre in the convent of the Geronomites at Granada was adorned with two hundred banners which he had taken. His envious rivals, and the treasurers of the kingdom of Naples in particular, induced the king in 1506 to demand a statement from Gonzalez of the use he had made of the great sums received from Spain for the conduct of the war in Italy ; and, in fact, the king was so small

as to consent, and even to be present on the occasion
of the conference.

"Gonzalez acceded to the demand with the
haughtiest disdain, and proposed to give a severe
lesson to the treasurers and the king upon the treat-
ment and consideration to be accorded a conqueror
of kingdoms.

"He replied with great indifference and calmness
that he would prepare his accounts for the following
day, and would let it appear which was the debtor,
himself or the exchequer, which demanded an account of one hundred and thirty thousand ducats
delivered upon the first payment, eighty thousand
crowns upon the second, three millions upon the
third, eleven millions upon the fourth, thirteen millions upon the fifth, and so on as the solemn, nasal,
foolish secretary who authorized so important an act
continued to enumerate the sums.

"The great Gonzalez kept his word, presented
himself at the second audience, and, bringing out a
voluminous book in which he had noted his justifica-
tion, he began with the following words in a deep,
sonorous voice :

" 'Two hundred thousand seven hundred and
thirty-six ducats and nine reales to the fathers, the
nuns, and the poor, to the end that they might pray
God for the triumph of the Spanish arms.

" 'One hundred thousand ducats for powder and
shot.

" ' Ten thousand ducats for perfumed gloves to protect the soldiers from the stench of the corpses of the enemy left on the field of battle.

" ' One hundred and seventy thousand ducats for renewing bells worn out by continuous ringing for constant new victories over the enemy.

" ' Fifty thousand ducats for brandy for the soldiers on the day of battle.

" ' A million and a half ducats for the maintenance of the prisoners and wounded.

" ' A million for returning thanks and Te Deums to the Omnipotent.

" ' Three hundred millions in masses for the dead.

" ' Seven hundred thousand four hundred and ninety-four ducats for spies and . . .

" ' One hundred millions for the patience which I showed yesterday on hearing that the king demanded an account from the man who has given him his kingdom.'

" These are the celebrated accounts of the great captain, the originals of which are in the possession of Count d'Altimira.

" One of the original accounts, with the autograph seal of the great captain, exists in the Military Museum of London, where it is guarded with great care."

On reading this document I returned to the hotel, making invidious comparisons between Gonzalez di Cordova and the Spanish generals of our times,

which, for grave state reasons, as they say in the
tragedies, I dare not repeat.

In the hotel I saw something new every day.
There were many university students who had come
from Malaga and other Andalusian cities to take the
examination for the doctor's degree at Granada,
whether because they were a little easier there or
for what other reason I do not know. We all ate
at a round table. One morning at breakfast one of
the students, a young man of about twenty, announced that at two o'clock he was to be examined
in canon law, and that, not feeling very sure of himself, he had decided to take a glass of wine to refresh
the springs of eloquence. He was accustomed to
drink only wine weakened with water, and committed the imprudence of emptying at a single
draught a glass of the vintage of Xerez. His face
changed in an instant in so strange a manner that if
I had not seen the transformation with my own eyes
I should not have believed that he was the same
person.

"There! that is enough!" cried his friends.

But the young man, who already felt that he had
become suddenly strong, keen, and confident, cast a
compassionate glance at his companions, and with
a lordly gesture ordered the waiter to fetch him
another glass.

"You will be drunk," they said.

His only response was to drain a second glass.

Then he became wonderfully talkative. There was a score of persons at table: in a few minutes he was conversing with them all, and he revealed a thousand secrets of his past life and his plans for the future. He said that he was from Cadiz, that he had eight thousand francs a year to spend, and that he wished to devote himself to a diplomatic career, because with that revenue, added to something which his uncle would leave him, he should be able to cut a good figure wherever he might be; that he had decided to take a wife at thirty, and to marry a woman as tall as himself, because it was his opinion that the wife should be of the same stature as her husband, to keep either from getting the upper hand of the other; that when he was a boy he was in love with the daughter of an American consul as beautiful as a flower and strong as a pine, but she had a red birth-mark behind one ear, which looked badly, although she knew how to cover it very well with her scarf, and he showed us with his napkin how she covered it; and that Don Amadeus was too ingenuous a man to succeed in governing Spain; that of the poets Zorilla and Espronceda, he had always preferred Espronceda; that it would be folly to cede Cuba to America; that the examination on canon law made him laugh; and that he wished to drink another four fingers of Xerez, the finest wine in Europe.

He drank a third glass in spite of the good coun-

sel and disapprobation of his friends, and after prat-
tling a little longer amid the laughter of his audience, he suddenly became silent, looked fixedly at a
lady sitting opposite to him, dropped his head, and
fell asleep. I thought that he could not present himself for the examination that day, but was mistaken.
A short hour later they awakened him; he went up
stairs to wash his face, ran off to the university still
drowsy, took his examination, and was promoted, to
the greater glory of the wine of Xerez and Spanish
diplomacy.

I devoted the following days to visiting the monuments, or, to be more accurate, the ruins of the
Moorish monuments which besides the Alhambra
and the Generalife attest the ancient splendor of
Granada. Insomuch as it was the last bulwark of
Islam, Granada is the city which presents the most
numerous relics of all the cities of Spain. On the
hill called the hill of *Dinadamar* (the Fountain of
Tears) one may still see the ruins of four towers
rising at the four corners of a great cistern into
which flowed the waters from the Sierra to supply
the highest part of the city. There were baths, gardens, and villas of which not a trace remains: from
that point one overlooked the city with its minarets,
its terraces, and its mosques gleaming among the
palms and cypresses. Near there one sees a Moorish gate called the gate of Elvira—a great arch
crowned with battlements—and beyond it are the

ruins of the palaces of the caliphs. Near the Alameda promenade stands a square tower in which there is a great hall ornamented with the usual Arabian inscriptions. Near the convent of San Domingo are the remains of gardens and palaces once joined to the Alhambra by a subterranean passage. Within the city is the Alcaiceria, a Moorish market almost perfectly preserved, formed of a few little streets as straight and narrow as corridors, lined with two rows of shops, one adjoining the other, and presenting the strange appearance of an Asiatic bazaar. In short, one cannot take a step in Granada without coming face to face with an arch, an arabesque, a column, or a pile of stones which suggests its fantastic, luxurious past.

What turns and windings have I not made through those tortuous streets at the hottest hour of the day, under a sun that shrivelled my brain, without meeting a living soul! At Granada, as in the other cities of Andalusia, the people are alive only at night, and the night repays them for the imprisonment of the day; the public promenades are crowded and confused by the hurry and jostling of a multitude, one half of which seems to be seeking the other half upon urgent business. The crowd is densest in the Alameda, but, for all that, I spent my evenings on the Alameda with Gongora, who talked to me of Moorish monuments, and with a journalist who discoursed on politics, and also with another

young man who talked of women, and frequently
with all three of them together, to my infinite
pleasure, because those cheery meetings, like those of
school-boys, at odd times and places, refreshed my
mind, to steal a beautiful simile, like a summer
shower refreshes the grass as it falls faster and
faster, dancing for joy.

If I were obliged to say something about the
people of Granada, I should be embarrassed, because
I have not seen them. In the day-time I met no
one in the streets, and at night I could not see them.
The theatres were not open, and when I might have
found some one in the city I was wandering through
the halls or avenues of the Alhambra; and then I
had so much to do to see everything in the short
time which I had allowed myself that no unoccupied
moments remained for those chance conversations,
like the ones I had in the other cities, in the streets
and the cafés, with whomever I happened to meet.

But from what I learned from men who were in
a position to give me trustworthy information, the
people of Granada do not enjoy an enviable reputation in Spain. They are said to be ill-tempered,
violent, vindictive, and bloodthirsty; and this ar-
raignment is not disproved by the pages of the city
newspapers. It is not publicly stated, but every one
knows it for a fact, that popular instruction in Granada is at a lower ebb than even in Seville and the
other smaller Spanish cities, and, as a rule, every-

thing that cannot be produced by the sun and the soil, which produce so bountifully, goes to the bad, either through indolence or ignorance or shiftlessness. Granada is not connected by railway with any important city: she lives alone, surrounded by her gardens, enclosed by her mountains, happy with the fruits which Nature produces under her hand, gently lulling herself to sleep in the vanity of her beauty and the pride of her history—idle, drowsy, and fanciful, content to answer with a yawn to any one who reproves her for her condition: "I gave Spain the painter Alonzo Cano, the poet Louis de Leon, the historian Fernando de Castillo, the sacred orator Luis di Grenada, and the minister Martinez de la Rosas. I have paid my debt, leave me in peace;" and this is the reply made by almost all the southern cities of Spain, more beautiful, alas! than wise and industrious, and proud rather than civilized. Ah! one who has seen them can never have done exclaiming, "What a pity!"

"Now that you have seen all the marvels of Moorish art and tropical vegetation there remains the suburb of the Albaicin to be seen before you can say that you know Granada. Prepare your mind for a new world, put your hand on your purse, and follow me."

So said Gongora to me on the last evening of my sojourn in Granada. A Republican journalist was with us, Melchiorre Almago by name, the director

of the *Idea*, a congenial, affable young man, who to
accompany us sacrificed his dinner and a leading
article that he had been cogitating since morning.

We walked on until we came to the square of the
Audiencia. There Gongora pointed out an alley
winding up a hill, and said to me, "Here commences the Albaicin;" and Señor Melchiorre, touching a house with his cane, added, "Here commences
the territory of the republic."

We turned up the alley, passed from it into another, and from that into a third, always ascending,
without my seeing anything extraordinary, although
I looked curiously in every direction. Narrow streets,
squalid houses, old women dozing on the doorsteps,
mothers carefully inspecting their children's heads,
gaping dogs, crowing cocks, ragged boys running
and shouting, and the other things that one always
sees in the suburbs; but in those streets nothing
more. But gradually, as we ascended, the appearance of the houses and the people began to change;
the roofs became lower, the windows fewer, the doors
smaller, and the people more ragged. In the middle
of every street ran a little stream in a walled gutter,
in the Moorish style; here and there over the doors
and around the windows one saw the remains of arabesques and fragments of columns, and in the corners of the squares fountains and well-curbs of the
time of the Moorish dominion. At every hundred
steps it seemed as if we had gone back fifty years

toward the age of the caliphs. My two companions
touched me on the elbow from time to time, saying
as they did so, "Look at that old woman!"—"Look
at that little girl!"—"Look at that man!" and I
looked, and asked, "Who are these people?" If I
had unexpectedly found myself in that place, I
should have believed on seeing those men and
women that I was in an African village, so strange
were the faces, the dress, the manner of moving,
talking, and looking, at so short a distance from the
centre of Granada—so different were they from the
people that I had seen up to that time. At every
turn I stopped to look in the face of my companions,
and they answered, "That is nothing; we are now
in the civilized part of the Albaicin; this is the
Parisian quarter of the suburb; let us go on."

We went on, and the streets seemed like the bed
of a torrent—paths hollowed out among the rocks,
all banks and gullies, broken and stony—some so
steep that a mule could not climb them, others so
narrow that a man could scarcely pass; some
blocked by women and children sitting on the
ground, others grass-grown and deserted; and all so
squalid, wild, and uncouth that the most wretched of
our villages cannot give one an idea of them, because this is a poverty that bears the impress of
another race and another continent. We turned
into a labyrinth of streets, passing from time to
time under a great Moorish arch or through a high

square from which one commanded a view of the wide valleys, the snow-covered mountains, and a part of the lower city, until finally we arrived at a street rougher and narrower than any we had yet seen; and there we stopped to take breath.

"Here commences the real Albaicin," said the young archeologist. "Look at that house!"

I looked; it was a low, smoke-stained, ruinous house, with a door that seemed like the mouth of a cavern, before which one saw, under a mass of rags, a group, or rather a heap, of old women and little children, who upon our approach raised their eyes heavy with sleep, and with bony hands removed from the threshold some filth which impeded our passage.

"Let us enter," said my friend.

"Enter?" I demanded.

If they had told me that beyond those walls there was a facsimile of the famous Court of Miracles which Victor Hugo has described, I should not have doubted their word. No door has ever said more emphatically than that, "Stand back!" I cannot find a better comparison than the gaping mouth of a gigantic witch breathing out pestilential vapors. But I took courage and entered.

Oh, marvellous! It was the court of a Moorish house surrounded by graceful little columns surmounted by lovely arches, with those indescribable traceries of the Alhambra along the porticoes and

around the mullioned windows, with the beams and
ceiling carved and enamelled with little niches for
vases of flowers and urns of perfume, with a pool
in the middle, and all the traces and memorials of
the delicate life of an opulent family. And in that
house lived those wretched people!

We went out and entered other houses, in all of
which I found some fragments of Moorish architecture and sculpture. From time to time Gongora
would say to me, "This was a harem. Those were
the baths of the women; up yonder was the chamber of a favorite;" and I fixed my eyes upon every
bit of the arabesqued wall and upon all the little
columns of the windows, as if to ask them for a revelation of their secrets only a name or a magic
word with which I might reconstruct in an instant
the ruined edifice and summon the beautiful Arabians who had dwelt there. But, alas! amid the
columns and under the arches of the windows there
were only rags and wrinkled faces.

Among other houses, we entered one where we
found a group of girls sewing under the shade of a
tree in the courtyard, directed by an old woman.
They were all working upon a great piece of cloth
that seemed like a mat or a bed-spread, in black and
gray stripes. I approached and asked one of the
girls, "What is this?"

They all looked up and with a concerted movement spread the cloth open, so that I could see their

work plainly. Almost before I had seen it I cried, "I will buy it."

They all began to laugh. It was the mantle of an Andalusian mountaineer, made to wear in the saddle, rectangular in form, with an opening in the middle to put one's head through, embroidered in bright-colored worsteds along the two shortest sides and around the opening. The design of the embroid-eries, which represented birds and fantastic flowers, green, blue, white, red, and yellow, all in a mass, was as crude as a pattern a child might make: the beauty of the work lay altogether in the harmony of the colors, which was truly marvellous. I cannot express the sensation produced by the sight of that mantle, except by saying that it laughed and filled one with its cheerfulness; and it seems to me im-possible to imagine anything gayer, more festive, or more childishly and gracefully capricious. It was a thing to look upon in order to bring yourself out of a bad humor, or when you wish to write a pretty verse in a lady's album, or when you are expecting a person whom you wish to receive with your brightest smile.

"When will you finish these embroideries?" I asked one of the girls.

" *Hoy mismo* " (to-day), they all replied in chorus.

" And what is the mantle worth?"

" *Cinco* " (five), stammered one.

The old women pierced her with a glance which

seemed to say, "Blockhead!" and answered hastily, "Six *duros*."

Six *duros* are thirty francs; it did not seem much to me, and I put my hand in my pocket.

Gongora cast a withering glance at me which seemed to say, "You simpleton!" and, drawing me back by the arm, said, "One moment: six *duros* is an exorbitant price."

The old woman shot him another glance which seemed to say, "Brigand!" and replied, "I cannot take less."

Gongora gave her another glance, which seemed to say, "Liar!" and said, "Come, now; you can take four *duros;* you would not ask more from the country-people."

The old woman insisted, and for a while we continued to exchange with our eyes the titles of simpleton, swindler, marplot, liar, pinch-penny, spendthrift, until the mantle was sold to me for five duros, and I paid and left my address, and we went out blessed and commended to God by the old woman and followed a good way by the black eyes of the embroiderers.

We went on from street to street, among houses increasingly wretched and growing blacker and blacker, and more revolting rags and faces. But we never came to the end, and I asked my companions, "Will you have the goodness to tell me if Granada has any limits, and if so where they are?

May one ask where we are going and how we shall return home?" But they simply laughed and went forward.

" Is there anything stranger than this to be seen?" I asked at a certain point.

" Stranger?" they both replied. " This second part of the suburb which you have seen still belongs to civilization: if not the Parisian, it is at least the Madrid, quarter of the Albaicin, and there *is* something else; let us go on."

We passed through a very small street containing some scantily-clothed women, who looked like people fallen from the moon; crossed a little square full of babies and pigs in friendly confusion; passed through two or three other alleys, now climbing, now descending, now in the midst of houses, now among piles of rubbish, now between trees and now among rocks, until we finally arrived at the solitary place on a hillside from which we saw in front the Generalife, to the right the Alhambra, and below a deep valley filled with a dense wood.

It was growing dark; no one was in sight and not a voice was heard.

" Is this the end of the suburb?" I asked.

My two companions laughed and said, " Look in that direction."

I turned and saw along the street that was lost in a distant grove an interminable row of houses. Of houses? Rather of dens dug in the earth, with a

bit of wall in front, with holes for windows and crev-
ices for doors, and wild plants of every sort on top
and along the sides—veritable caves of beasts, in
which by the glow of faint lights, scarcely visible,
swarmed the gypsies by hundreds; a people multiplying in the bowels of the mountain, poorer, blacker, and
more savage than any seen before; another city,
unknown to the greater part of Granada, inaccessible to the police, closed to the census-officers, ignorant of every law and of all government, living
one knows not how, how numerous no one knows,
foreign to the city, to Spain, and to modern civilization, with a language and statutes and manners of
their own—superstitious, false, thieving, beggarly,
and fierce.

"Button up your coat and look out for your
watch," said Gongora to me, "and let us go forward."

We had not taken a hundred steps when a half-
naked boy, black as the walls of his hovel, ran out,
gave a cry, and, making a sign to the other boys
who followed him, dashed toward us; behind the
boys came the women; behind the women the men,
and then old men, old women, and more children;
and in less time than it takes to tell it we were surrounded by a crowd. My two friends, recognized as
Granadines, succeeded in saving themselves; I was
left in the lurch. I can still see those horrid faces,
still hear those voices, and still feel the pressure of

those hands: gesticulating, shouting, saying a thousand things which I did not understand; dragging at
my coat, my waistcoat, and my sleeves, they pressed
upon me like a pack of famished people, breathed in
my face, and cut off my very breath. They were,
for the most part, half naked and emaciated—their
garments falling in tatters, with unkempt hair, horrible to see; I seemed to be like Don Roderick in
the midst of a crowd of the infected in that famous
dream of the August night.

"What do these people want?" I asked myself.
"Where have I been brought? How shall I get out
of this?" I felt almost a sense of fear, and looked
around uneasily. Little by little I began to understand.

"I have a sore on my shoulder," said one; "I
cannot work; give me a penny."

"I have a broken leg," said another.

"I have a palsied arm,"

"I have had a long sickness."

"*Un cuarto, Señorito!*"

"*Un real, caballero!*"

"*Una peseta para todos!*"

This last request was received with a general cry
of approval: "*Una peseta para todos!*" (a *peseta* for
us all).

With some little trepidation I drew out my purse;
they all stood on tiptoe; the nearest poked their
chins into it; those behind put their chins on the

heads of those in front; the farthest stretched out their arms.

"One moment," I cried. "Who has the most authority among you all?"

They all replied with one voice, stretching out their arms toward the same person, "That one."

It was a terrible old hag, all nose and chin, with a great tuft of white hair standing straight above her head like a bunch of feathers, and a mouth which seemed like a letter-box, with little clothing save a chemise—black, shrivelled, and mummified; she approached me bowing and smiling, and held out her hands to take mine.

"What do you want?" I demanded, taking a step backward.

"Your fortune," they all cried.

"Tell my fortune, then," I replied, holding out my hand.

· The old woman took my poor hand between her ten—I cannot say fingers, but shapeless bones—placed her sharp nose on it, raised her head, looked hard at me, pointed her finger toward me, and, swaying and pausing at every sentence as if she were reciting poetry, said to me in inspired accents, "Thou wert born upon a famous day.

"Upon a famous day also shalt thou die.

"Thou art the possessor of amazing riches."

Here she muttered I know not what about sweethearts and marriage and felicity, from which I understood that she supposed I was married, and then she continued : " On the day of thy marriage there was great feasting in thy house ; there were many to give and take.

" And another woman wept.

" And when thou seest her the wings of thy heart open."

And so on in this strain, saying that I had sweet-hearts and friends and treasures and jewels in store for me every day of the year, in every country of the world. While the old woman was speaking they were all silent, as if they believed she had prophesied truly. She finally closed her prophecy with a formula of dismissal, and ended the formula by extending her arms and making a skip in a dancing attitude. I gave her the peseta, and the crowd broke into shouting, applause, and singing, making a thousand uncanny hops and gestures around me, saluting me with nudges and slaps of the hand on my back, as if I were an old friend, until finally, by dint of wriggling and striking now one and then another, I succeeded in opening a passage and rejoined my friends. But a new danger threatened us. The news of the arrival of a foreigner had spread, the tribes were in motion, the city of the gypsies was all in an uproar; from the neighboring houses and from the distant huts, from the top of the hill and the bottom of the valley, ran boys, women with babies about their necks, old men with canes, cripples, and professional imposters, septuagenarian prophetesses who wished to tell my fortune—an army of beggars coming upon us from every direction. It was night; there was no time for hesitation; we broke into a run toward the city like school-boys. Then a devilish cry broke out behind us, and the nimblest began to chase us. Thanks to Heaven! after a short race we found ourselves in safety—tired and breathless, and covered with dust, but safe.

"It was necessary to escape at any cost," said Señor Melchiorre with a laugh; "otherwise we should have gone home without our shirts."

"And take notice," added Gongora, "that we have seen only the door of Gypsy-town, the civilized part, not the Paris nor the Madrid, but at least the Granada, of the Albaicin. If we could only have gone on! if you could have seen the rest!"

"But how many thousand are there of those people?" I demanded.

"No one knows."

"How do they live?"

"No one can imagine."

"What authority do they recognize?"

"One only—*los reyes* (the kings), the heads of families or of houses, those who have the most money and years. They never go out of their city; they know nothing, they live in the dark as to all that happens beyond the circle of their hovels. Dynasties fall, governments change, armies clash, and it is a miracle if the news ever reaches their ears. Ask them if Isabella is still on the throne; they do not know. Ask them who Amadeus is; they have never heard his name. They are born and perish like flies, and they live as they lived centuries ago, multiplying without leaving their own boundaries, ignorant and unknown, seeing nothing all their lives beyond the valleys lying below their feet and the Alhambra towering above their heads."

We passed again through all the streets that we had traversed, now dark and deserted, and endless as it seemed to me; and, climbing and descending, turning and twisting, and turning again, we finally arrived at the square of the Audiencia in the middle of the city of Granada—in the civilized world. At the sight of the brightly-lighted cafés and shops I experienced a feeling of pleasure, as if I had just returned to city-life after a year's sojourn in an uninhabited wilderness.

On the evening of the next day I left for Valencia. I remember that a few moments before starting, as I was paying my hotel-bill, I observed to the proprietor that there was an overcharge for one candle, and playfully asked him, "Will you deduct it for me?" The proprietor seized his pen, and, deducting twenty centimes from the total charge, replied in a voice which he wished to appear emotional, "The devil! among Italians!"

VALENCIA.

Vol. II.—17

VALENCIA.

THE journey from Granada to Valencia, made all *de un tiron* (at one breath), as they say in Spain, is one of those recreations in which a rational man indulges only once in his life. From Granada to Menjibar, a village on the left bank of the Guadalquivir, between Jaen and Andujar, is a night's ride by diligence; from Menjibar to the Alcazar de San Juan is a half-day's journey by railway in an uncurtained carriage, through a plain as bare as the palm of one's hand, under a blazing sun; and from the Alcazar de San Juan to Valencia, taking account of an entire evening spent in the station of the Alcazar, makes another night and another morning before one reaches the longed-for city at noon, where Nature, as Emile Praga would say, is horrified at the dreadful idea that there are still four months of summer.

But it must be said that the country through which one passes is so beautiful from beginning to the end that if one were capable of appreciation when one is dead with sleep and finds one's self turning into water by reason of the heat, one would

259

go into ecstasies a thousand times. It is a journey
of unexpected landscapes, sudden vistas, remarkable
contrasts, theatrical effects of Nature, so to speak—
marvellous and fantastic transformations, which leave
in the mind an indescribable, vague illusion of having passed not through a part of Spain, but along an
entire meridian of the earth across the most dissim-
ilar countries. From the *vega* of Granada, which
you cross in the moonlight, almost opening a way
among the groves and gardens, in the midst of a
luxuriant vegetation that seems to crowd around
you like a tossing sea, ready to overflow and engulf
you with its billows of verdure,—from this you
emerge into the midst of ragged and precipitous
mountains, where not a trace of human habitation
is to be seen; you graze the edge of precipices, wind
along the banks of mountain-torrents, run along at
the bottom of the ravines, and seem to be lost in a
rocky labyrinth. Then you come out a second time
among the green hills and flowery fields of upper
Andalusia, and then, all suddenly, the fields and hills
disappear and you find yourself in the midst of the
rocky mountains of the Sierra Morena, that hang
over your head from every direction and close the
horizon all around like the walls of an immense
abyss. You leave the Sierra Morena, and the desert
plains of La Mancha stretch before you; you leave
La Mancha and advance through the flowery plain
of Almansa, varied by every sort of cultivation,

presenting the appearance of a vast carpet of checkered pattern colored in all the shades of green that
can be found upon the pallet of a landscape-painter.
And, finally, the plain of Almansa opens into a delightful oasis, a land blest of God, a true earthly
paradise, the kingdom of Valencia, from whose
boundaries, even to the city itself, you pass through
gardens, vineyards, fragrant orange-groves, white
villas encircled by terraces, cheerful, brightly-colored villages, clusters, avenues, and groves of palms,
pomegranates, aloes, and sugar-canes, interminable
hedges of Indian fig, long chains of low hills, and
conical mounds cultivated as kitchen-gardens and
flower-beds, laid out with minute care from top to
bottom, and variegated like great bunches of grass
and flowers; and everywhere a vigorous vegetation
which hides every bare spot, covers every height,
clothes every projection, climbs, falls, trails along,
marches forward, overflows, intertwines, shuts off
the view, impedes the road, dazzles with its verdure,
wearies with its beauty, confounds with its caprices
and its frolics, and produces an effect as of a sudden
parting of the earth raised to fever heat by the fires
of a secret volcano.

The first building which meets the eye on entering
Valencia is an immense bull-ring situated to the right
of the railway. The building consists of four orders
of superimposed arches rising on stout pilasters, all
of brick, and in the distance resembling the Colos-

seum. It is the bull-ring where on the fourth of
September, 1871, King Amadeus, in the presence of
thousands of spectators, shook hands with Tato, the
celebrated one-legged *torero*, who as director of the
spectacle had asked permission to render his homage
in the royal box. Valencia is full of mementos of
the duke d'Aosta. The sacristan of the cathedral
has in his possession a gold chronometer bearing the
duke's initials in diamonds, with a chain of pearls,
which was presented by him when he went to pray
in the chapel of Our Lady of the Desolate. In the
hospice of the same name the poor remember that
one day they received their daily bread from his
hand. In the mosaic workshop of one Nolla they
preserve two bricks, upon one of which he cut his
own name with his sword, and upon the other the
name of the queen. In the Plaza di Tetuan the
people point out the house of Count di Cervellon,
where he was entertained; it is the same house in
which Ferdinand VII. signed the decrees annulling
the constitution in 1814, in which Queen Christina
abdicated the throne in 1840, in which Queen Isabella spent some days in 1858. In short, there is
not a corner of the city of which it cannot be said,
Here he shook hands with a working-man, here he
visited a factory, there he passed on foot far from
his suite, surrounded by a crowd, trustful, serene,
and smiling.

It was in Valencia, since I am speaking of the

duke d'Aosta,—it was in the city of Valencia that a little girl of five years in reciting some verses touched upon that terrible subject of a *foreign king* with probably the noblest and most considerate words spoken in Spain for many years previous to that time—words which, if all Spain had remembered and pondered then, would perhaps have spared her many of those calamities which have befallen her, and others which still threaten; words which perhaps one day some Spaniard may repeat with a sigh, and which already at this time draw from events a marvellous light of truth and beauty. And, since these verses are graceful and simple, I transcribe them here. The poem is entitled " God and the King," and runs as follows:

> " Dios, en todo soberano,
> Creò un dia á los mortales,
> Y á todos nos hizo iguales
> Con su poderosa mano.

> " No reconoció Naciones
> Ni colores ni matices?
> Y en ver los hombres felices
> Cifró sus aspiraciones.

> " El Rey, che su imágen es,
> Su bondad debe imitar
> Y el pueblo no ha de indagar
> Si es aleman ó francés.

> " Porqué con ceño iracundo
> Rechazarle siendo bueno?
> Un Rey de bondades lleno
> Tiene por su patria el mundo.

"Vino de nacion estraña
  Cárlos Quinto emperador,
  Y conquistó su valor
  Mil laureles para España.

"Y es un recuerdo glorioso
  Aunque en guerra cimentado,
  El venturoso reinado
  De Felipe el Animoso.

"Hoy el tercero sois vos
  Nacido en estraño suelo
  Que viene á ver nuestro cielo
  Puro destello de Dios.

"Al rayo de nuestro sol
  Sed bueno, justo y leal,
  Que á un Rey bueno y liberal
  Adora el pueblo español.

"Y á vuestra frente el trofeo
  Ceñid de perpetua gloria,
  Para que diga la historia
  —Fué grande el Rey Amadeo."

"God, Ruler over all, created mortals one day, and made all equal with His mighty hand. He recognized neither nations nor colors nor divisions, and to behold men happy was His desire. The king, who is His image, ought to imitate His goodness, and the people have no need to ask whether he be German or French. Why, then, with angry frown repulse him if he be good? A king abounding in good deeds holds the world as his country. Charles V., the emperor, came from a foreign nation, and by his valor won a thousand laurels for Spain. And the fortunate reign of Philip the Courageous is a glorious memory even though founded upon war.

"To-day a third king rules you born on a foreign soil, who comes to look upon our sky, a clear spark of God. His love is true and just and loyal to the light of our sun, and this is a good and liberal king the Spanish people adore. And around your brows you shall wear the trophy of perpetual glory upon which history shall write, 'Great was King Amadeus.'"

Oh, poor little girl! how many wise things you have said! and how many foolish things others have done!

The city of Valencia, if one enters it with one's mind full of the ballads in which the poets sang of its marvels, does not seem to correspond to the lovely image formed of it; neither, on the other hand, does it offer that sinister appearance for which one is prepared if one considers its just fame as a turbulent, warlike city, the fomenter of civil strife— a city prouder of the smell of its powder than of the fragrance of its orange-groves. It is a city built in the midst of a vast flowery plain on the right bank of the Guadalquivir, which separates it from the suburbs, a little way from the roadstead which serves as a port, and consists all of tortuous streets lined with high, ungainly, many-colored houses, and on this account less pleasing in appearance than the streets of the Andalusian cities, and entirely devoid of that evasive Oriental grace which so strangely stirs one's fancy. Along the left bank of the river extends a magnificent promenade formed of majestic avenues and beautiful gardens. These one reaches by going out of the city through the gate of the Cid, a structure flanked by two great embattled towers named after the hero because he passed through it in 1094 after he had expelled the Moors from Valencia. The cathedral, built upon the spot where stood a temple of Diana in Roman times, then a church of San Salvador in the time of the Goths, then a mosque in Moorish times, afterward converted into a church by the Cid, changed a second time into a mosque by the Moors in 1101, and for the third time into a church by King Don Jayme after the final overthrow of the invaders, is a vast structure, exceedingly rich in ornaments and treasures, but it cannot bear comparison with the greater number of the other Spanish cathedrals. There are a few palaces worth seeing, besides the palace of the Audiencia, a beautiful monument of the sixteenth century in which the Cortes of the kingdom of Valencia assembled; the *Casa de Ayuntamiento*, built between the fifteenth and sixteenth centuries, in which are preserved the sword of Don Jayme, the keys of the çity, and the banner of the Moors; and, above all, *the Lonja*—the Bourse of the merchants—notable for its celebrated hall consisting of three great naves divided by twenty-four spiral columns, above which curve the light arches of the vaulted roof in bold lines, the architecture imparting to the eye a pleasing impression of gayety and harmony. And, finally, there is the art-gallery, which is not one of the least in Spain.

But, to tell the truth, in those few days that I remained at Valencia waiting for the boat I was more occupied by politics than by art. And I proved the truth of the words I heard an illustrious Italian say before I left Italy—one who knew Spain like his his own home: "The foreigner who lives even for a short time in Spain is drawn little by little, almost insensibly, to heat his blood and muddle his brain over politics, as if Spain were his own country or as if the fortunes of his country were depending upon those of Spain. The passions are so inflamed, the struggle is so furious, and in this struggle there is always so clearly at stake the future, the safety, and the life of the nation, that it is impossible for any one with the least tinge of the Latin blood in his imagination and his system to remain an indifferent spectator. You must needs grow excited, speak at party meetings, take the elections seriously, mingle with the crowd at the political demonstrations, break with your friends, form a clique of those who think as you think—make, in a word, a Spaniard of yourself, even to the whites of your eyes. And gradu-

ally, as you become Spanish, you forget Europe, as
if it were at the antipodes, and end in seeing nothing
beyond Spain, as if you were governing it, and as if
all its interests were in your hands."

Such is the case, and this was my experience. In
those few days the Conservative ministry was ship-
wrecked and the Radicals had the wind behind
them. Spain was all in a ferment; governors, generals, officials of all grades and of all administra-
tions fell; a crowd of parvenus burst into the offices
of the ministry with cries of joy: Zorilla was to in-
augurate a new era of prosperity and peace; Don
Amadeus had had an inspiration from heaven; liberty had conquered; Spain was saved. And I, as I
listened to the band playing in front of the new gov-
vernor's mansion under a clear starry sky in the
midst of a joyous crowd,—I too had a ray of hope
that the throne of Don Amadeus might finally extend its roots, and reproached myself for being too
prone to predict evil. And that comedy which
Zorilla played at his villa when he would by no
means accept the presidency of the ministry, and
sent back his friends and the members of the depu-
tation, and finally, tired of continually saying no,
fell into a swoon on saying yes,—this, I say, gave
me at the time a high opinion of the firmness of his
character and led me to augur happily for the new
government. And I said to myself that it was a sin
to leave Spain just when the horizon was clearing

and the royal palace of Madrid was tinted rose-color.
And I had already considered the plan of returning
to Madrid that I might have the satisfaction of sending some consoling news to Italy, and so be pardoned
for the imprudence of sending unvarnished accounts
of the situation up to that time. And I repeated
the verses of Prati:

> "Oh qual destin t'aspetta
> Aquila giovenetta!"

(Oh what a destiny awaits thee, young eagle!)
And, save a little bombast in the appellation, it
seemed to me that they contained a prophecy, and
I imagined meeting the poet in the Piazza Colonna
at Rome and running toward him to offer my con-
gratulations and press his hand. . . .

The most beautiful sight in Valencia is the market. The Valencian peasants are the most artistic
and bizarre in their dress of all the peasants of
Spain. To cut a good figure in a group of maskers
at one of our masquerades they need only enter the
theatre dressed as they would be on a festival or
market-day in the streets of Valencia and along
the country roads. On first seeing them dressed in
this style, one laughs, and cannot in any way be
brought to believe that they are Spanish peasants.
They have an indescribable air of Greeks, Bedouins,
buffoons, tightrope-walkers, women partly undressed
on their way to bed, the silent characters of a play

not quite ready to make their appearance, or facetious people who wish to make themselves generally
ridiculous. They wear a full white shirt that takes
the place of a jacket; a parti-colored velvet waistcoat open at the breast; a pair of zouave linen
breeches which do not reach the knee, looking like
drawers and standing out like the skirts of a ballet-
dancer; a red or blue sash around the waist; a sort
of embroidered white woollen stockings that leave
the knee bare; a pair of corded sandals like those
of the Catalan peasants; and on their heads, which
are almost all shaved like those of the Chinese,
they wear a handkerchief, red, sky-blue, yellow, or white, bound around like a cornucopia, and
knotted at the temples or at the nape of the neck.
They sometimes wear small velvet hats similar in
shape to those worn in the other provinces of Spain.
When they go into the city they nearly all carry
around their shoulders or on their arms, now like a
shawl, now like a mantle, or again like a little cape,
a woollen *capa*, long and narrow, in brightly-colored
stripes in which white and red predominate, adorned
with fringe and rosettes. One may easily imagine
the appearance presented by a square where there
are gathered some hundreds of men dressed after
this fashion: it is a Carnival scene, a festival, a tumult of colors, that makes one feel as gay as a band
of music; a spectacle at once clownish, pretty, imposing, and ridiculous, to which the haughty faces

and the majestic bearing which distinguish the Valencian peasants add an air of gravity which heightens the extraordinary beauty of the scene.

If there is an insolent, lying proverb, it is that old Spanish one which says, "In Valencia flesh is grass, grass is water, men are women, and the women nothing." Leaving that part about the flesh and the grass, which is a pun, the men, especially those of the lower classes, are tall and robust, and have the bold appearance of the Catalans and Arragonese, with a livelier and more luminous expression of the eye; and the women, by the consent of all the Spaniards and of as many foreigners as have travelled in Spain, are the most classically beautiful in the country. The Valencians, who know that the eastern coast of the Peninsula was originally settled by Greeks and Carthaginians, say, "It is a clear case. The Grecian type of beauty has lingered here." I do not venture to say yes or no to this assertion, for to describe the beauty of the women of a city where one has passed only a few hours would seem to me like a license to be taken only by the compiler of a "Guide." But one can easily discover a decided difference between the Andalusian and Valencian types of beauty. The Valencian is taller, more robust, and fairer, with more regular features, gentler eyes, and a more matronly walk and carriage. She does not possess the bewitching air of the Andalusian, which makes it necessary to bite one's finger as if to subdue the sudden and alarming insurrection of one's capricious desires at sight of her; but the Valencian is a woman whom one regards with a feeling of calmer admiration, and while one looks one says, as La Harpe said of the Apollo Belvidere, "*Notre tete se releve, notre maintien s'ennoblit*," and instead of imagining a little Andalusian house to hide her from the eyes of the world, one longs for a marble palace to receive the ladies and cavaliers who will come to render her homage.

If one is to believe the rest of the Spaniards, the Valencian people are fierce and cruel beyond all imagination. If one wishes to get rid of an enemy, he finds an obliging man who for a few crowns undertakes the business with as much indifference as he would accept a commission to carry a letter to the post. A Valencian peasant who finds that he has a gun in his hands as he passes an unknown man in a lonely street says to his companion, " See if I can aim straight?" and takes aim and fires. This actually occurred not many years ago: I was assured of its truth. In the cities and villages of Spain the boys and young men of the people are accustomed to play at being bulls, as they call it. One takes the place of the bull and does the butting; another, with a sharp stick under his arm like a lance, climbs on the back of a third, who represents the horse, and repulses the assaults of the first. Once a band of

young Valencians thought they would introduce
some innovations into this sport, and so make it
seem a little more realistic and afford the spectators and the participants a little more amusement
than the customary way of playing it; and the innovations were to substitute for the stick a long
sharp-pointed knife, one of those formidable *navajas*
that we saw at Seville, and to give the man who took
the part of the bull two other shorter knives, which,
fastened firmly on either side of his head, answered
the purpose of horns. It seems incredible, but it is
true. They played with the knives, shed a sea of
blood, several were killed, some were mortally
wounded, and others badly hurt, without the game
becoming a fight, without the rules of the sport
being transgressed, and without any one raising his
voice to end the slaughter.

I tell these things as they were told to me,
although I am far from believing all that is said
against the Valencians; but it is certain that at Valencia the public safety, if not a myth, as our papers
poetically say in speaking of Romagna and Sicily, is
certainly not the first of the good things which one
enjoys after the blessing of life. I was persuaded
of this fact the first evening of my stay in the city.
I did not know the way to the port, but thought I
was near it, and asked a shop-woman which way I
should take. She uttered a cry of astonishment:

" Do you wish to go to the port, *caballero* ?"

"Yes."

"*Ave Maria purissima!* to the port at this hour?"

And she turned toward a group of women who were standing by the door, and said to them in the Valencian dialect, "Women, do you answer for me: this gentleman is asking me the way to the port!"

The women replied in one voice, "God save him!"

"But from what?"

"Don't risk yourself, sir."

"What is your reason?"

"A thousand reasons."

"Tell me one of them?"

"You would be murdered."

One reason was enough for me, as any one can imagine, and I did not go to the port.

For the rest, at Valencia as elsewhere, in whatever intercourse I had with the people I met only with courtesy as a foreigner and as an Italian—a friendly welcome even among those who would not hear foreign kings discussed in general, and princes of the house of Savoy in particular, and such men were numerous, but they were courteous enough to say at once, "Let us not harp on that string." To a foreigner who, when asked whence he comes, replies, "I am a Frenchman," they respond with an agreeable smile, as if to say, "We recognize each other." To one who answers, "I am a German or an Englishman," they make a slight inclination of the head, which implies, "I bow to you;" but when one replies, "I

am an Italian," they eagerly extend the hand as if
to say, "We are friends;" and they look at one with
an air of curiosity, as you look for the first time at a
person who is said to resemble you, and they smile
pleasantly on hearing the Italian tongue, as you
would smile on hearing some one, though in no
mocking spirit, imitate your voice and accents. In
no country in the world does an Italian feel nearer
home than in Spain. The sky, the speech, the
faces, and the dress remind him of his fatherland;
the veneration with which the Spanish pronounce
the names of our great poets and our great painters,
that vague and pleasing sense of curiosity with
which they speak of our famous cities, the enthusiasm with which they cultivate our music, the impul-
siveness of their affections, the fire of their language,
the rhythms of their poetry, the eyes of their women,
the air and the sun,—oh! an Italian must be without
a spark of love for his fatherland who does not feel
an emotion of sympathy for this country, who does
not feel inclined to excuse its errors, who does not
sincerely deplore its misfortunes, who does not desire for it a happy future. O beautiful hills of Valencia, smiling banks of the Guadalquivir, charmed
gardens of Granada, little white cottages of Seville,
proud towers of Toledo, roaring streets of Madrid,
and venerable walls of Saragossa! and you, kindly
hosts and courteous companions of my travels—you
who have spoken to me of Italy as of a second

fatherland, who with your festal gayety have scattered my restless melancholy!—I shall always carry deep down in my heart a feeling of gratitude and love for you, and I shall cherish your images in my memory, as one of the dearest recollections of my youth, and shall always think of you as one of the loveliest dreams of my life.

I repeated these words to myself at midnight as I looked over brightly-lighted Valencia, leaning against the rail of the good ship *Xenil*, which was on the point of sailing. Some young Spaniards had come on board with me. They were going to Marseilles to take ship from that port to the Antilles, where they expected to remain for some years. One of them stood alone weeping; suddenly he raised his head and looked toward the shore between two anchored vessels, and exclaimed in a tone of desolaton, "Oh, my God! I hoped she would not come!"

In a few moments a boat approached the ship; a little white figure, followed by a man enveloped in a cloak, hastily climbed the ladder, and with a deep sob threw herself into the arms of the young man, who had run to meet her.

At that moment the boatswain called, "All off, gentlemen!"

Then there followed a most distressing scene: the two young persons were torn apart, and the young lady was borne almost fainting to the boat, which pushed off a little and remained motionless.

The ship started.

The young man dashed madly forward toward the rail, and, sobbing, cried in a voice that pierced one's heart, "Adieu, darling! adieu! adieu!"

The little white figure stretched out her arms and perhaps responded, but her voice was not heard. The boat was dropped behind and disappeared.

One of the young men said to me in a whisper, "They are betrothed."

It was a lovely night, but sad. Valencia was soon lost to view, and I thought I should never see Spain again, and wept.

END OF VOL. II.

INDEX.

portrait of, 178; mementoes of, ii. 103.

Columbus, Ferdinand, history of, ii. 115; library of, ii, 118; note on his father's annotations, ii. 118; tomb of, ii. 114.

Concerts at Madrid, 173.

Conde, Henry II. de Bourbon, prince de, sword of, 176.

Conservative party, 96.

Consuelo the beautiful, ii. 81.

Consul, seeking the protection of the, ii. 106.

Convents: Angels, Granada, ii. 235; Cartuja, Granada, ii. 235; of the Escurial, 268; Santo Domingo, Granada, ii. 235; San Pablo, Valladolid, 134.

Cook, Capt. James, cane of, 180.

Cookery, Spanish, 14, 160; ii. 223.

Cordova, arrival at, ii. 62; at night, ii. 80; cathedral, ii. 74; Consuelo the beautiful, ii. 81; departed glory, ii. 62; impressions of, ii. 67; mosque, ii. 68; patio, a, ii. 65; pearl of the Orient, ii. 66; preaching the Holy War, ii. 75; relics of the past, ii. 80; streets of, ii. 64.

Cordova, General de, at Saragossa, 84.

Corregio, Antonio Allegri da, painting by, at Madrid, 182.

Cortes, the, 274; deputies, 274; oratorical displays, 275.

Cortez, Hernando, portrait of, 178; sword of, 176.

Cosa, Juan de la, map by, at Madrid, 178.

Costumes of peasantry: Andalusian, ii. 100; Catalan, 18; Cordovan, ii. 58; Granadan, ii. 189; Madrid, 165; Saragossan, 56; Valencian, ii. 270.

Country houses, ii. 100.

Courts: Lions, Alhambra, ii. 201; Myrtles, Alhambra, ii. 194; Oranges, Seville, ii. 115.

Court-life under Amadeus, 198.

Courtesy inherent in the Spanish people, 53, 290.

Cuco the matador, 207; ii. 94.

Currency, Spanish, 118.

Custejon, 92.

Customs officials, 14, 95.

Cybele, fountain of, at Madrid, 166.

D.

"Daggers," ii. 55.

Daguet, paintings by, at Madrid, 182.

"Dance de los seises," ii. 112.

Darro, the, ii. 213.

Democratic party, 96.

Democratic Progressionist party, 96, 97.

Deronda, Francisco Romero, the torero, 235.

Dialects: Andalusian, ii. 93; Arragonese, 55; Barcelonian, 20; Castilian, 55; Catalan, 15, 39; Madrid, 158; Perpignan, 12; Valencian, ii. 275; Valladolid, 132.

Dinadamar, hill of, ii. 240.

Discoveries, cabinet of, Naval Museum, Madrid, 177.

Djihad, or Holy War, ii. 76.

Domenichino, paintings by, at Madrid, 182.

Dominoes, popularity of game of, 31.

Don Quixote on Barcelona, 42; popularity of, 286; true to life, ii. 57.

Door-keys in Madrid, 171.

Drama, 169.

Drunkenness rare in Spain, 162.

Dumas, Alexandre, on Spanish cookery, 160.

Dürer, Albert, paintings by, at Madrid, 182.

E.

Ebro, commerce on the, 51; description of, 92.

Economist party, 96.

Education in Granada, ii. 242.

Egon ad Agoncilla, ruins of, 91.

Elpidius, bishop of Toledo, ii. 27.

Elvira Gate, Granada, ii. 240.

Escurial, the, arrival at, 258; altar of Santa Forma, 264; cell of Philip II., 261; church, 262; convent, 268; courtyard, 261; gardens, 272; gloominess, 273; history of, 260; holy relics, 272;

Manzoni, Alessandro, 189.
Margall, Pi y, political leader, 96; oratory of, 276.
Maria, granddaughter of Ferdinand and Isabella, tomb of, ii. 234.
Maria Louisa of Savoy tomb of, 266.
Marini, Giambattista, influence on Italian poetry, ii. 92.
Markets: Granada, ii. 241; Madrid, 174; Valencia, ii. 269; Valladolid, 132.
Marseilles, 11.
Martina the torera, 238.
Martinez de la Rosa, Francisco, 282; ii. 243; exiled in London, 65; quotation from, ii. 185.
Martos, political leader, 96; oratory of, 226.
Mascagni, Donato, paintings by, at Valladolid, 143.
Masked balls, 86.
May, second of, funeral memorial ceremonies, 243; monument to, 247.
Medina Az-Zahra, ii. 88.
Medina-Coeli, family, owners of the Casa de Pilato, ii. 136.
Mena, Juan de, "Labyrinth," ii. 92; popularity of, 287; street of, ii. 92.
Menendez, paintings by, at Madrid, 193.
Mengs, Anton Rafael, paintings by, at Madrid, 193.
Menjibar, ii. 259.
Merced, marquis de, 207.
Merriones, Gen., victories over Carlists, 288.
Michelangelo, Buonarotti, Cespede's tribute to, ii. 90; paintings by, at Burgos, 109; at Madrid, 182.
Mihrab of mosque of Cordova, ii. 72.
Military Museum of London possesses Gonzalez di Cordova's fiscal accounts, ii. 237.
Militia system, 202.
Mirabeau, Victor Hugo's description of, ii. 107.
Miranda, 94.
Moderate party, 96, 97.
Monastery of Montserrat, 46.

Monegro, Battista, statue by, 262.
Montegna, paintings by, at Seville, ii. 109.
Montpensier gardens, Seville, ii. 117, ii. 127; palace, ii. 104.
Montpensier, duke of, at Madrid, 197; party, 96, 97.
Montserrat, description of, 45; excursion to, 46; monastery of, 46.
Monzon, 50; castle, 51.
Moorish art, ii. 207; ruins, ii. 240.
Morales, Ambrosio, born in Cordova, ii. 90.
Moret, political leader, 96.
Moreto, Don Augustin, dramatist, 169.
Mosque of Cordova, ii. 68; of the Alhambra, ii. 216.
Mozarabe chapel, Toledo, ii. 29.
Mulato, paintings by, at Seville, ii. 109, ii 132.
Murat, Joachim, 50.
Murillo, Bartolomé Esteban, a painter of saints and virgins, 191; death of, ii. 100; estimate of his genius, 192; last painting, ii. 163; mementoes of, ii. 103; painting by, at Granada, ii. 235; at Madrid, 182, 183; at Seville, ii. 109, ii. 129; statue at Madrid, 156, 292.

N.

Naples, king of, demands an accounting from Gonzalez di Cordova, ii. 235.
Navagero, Andrea, influences poetry of Boscan, 37.
Navajas, ii. 136.
Navarrete, battle of, 91.
Navarrete, Juan Fernandez (El Mudo), paintings by, at Madrid, 193; at the Escurial, 263.
News from Spain, 10.
Newspapers hostile to Amadeus, 93, 200.
Nun, the flirting, 53.
Nunes, Duke Ferdinand, at the bull-fight, 209.
Night journey to Aranjuez, ii. 9; to Barcelona, 13; to Burgos, 97; to Cadiz, ii. 149; to Cordova, ii. 55; to Granada, ii. 181.

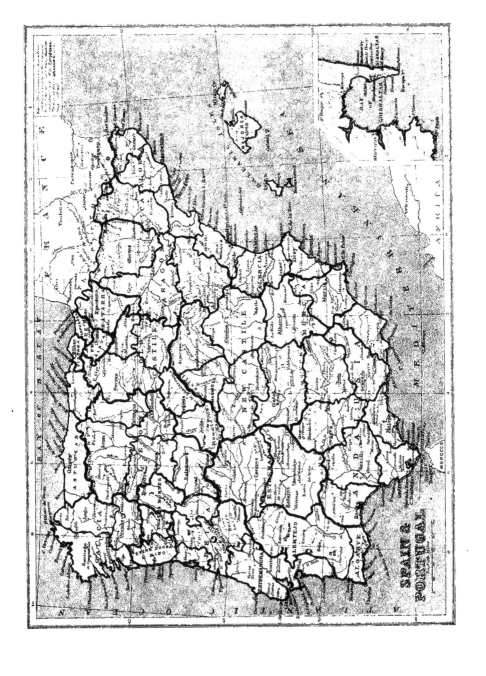

SPAIN & PORTUGAL

Lightning Source UK Ltd.
Milton Keynes UK
UKHW010720031218
333381UK00011B/1340/P